PRAISE FOR T

MURDER MOST SCOTTISH

A DEAD COLD MYSTERY

BLAKE BANNER

RIGHTHOUSE

ISBN-13: 978-1-63696-011-1

ISBN-10: 1-63696-011-1

Cover design by: Damonza

Printed in the United States of America

www.righthouse.com

www.instagram.com/righthousebooks

www.facebook.com/righthousebooks

twitter.com/righthousebooks

DEAD COLD MYSTERY SERIES

ONE

We'd touched down in Edinburgh at 7:10 a.m. local time, collected a large, characterless vehicle from the car hire centre, and, resisting the temptation to explore Edinburgh, we took the M90, crossed the Firth of Forth over the spectacular Forth Road Bridge as the sun climbed over the North Sea, and headed north, toward the wild and remote north coast of Scotland, in the Scottish Highlands.

I drove first, and Dehan sat back and watched the strange, conflicted landscape that was at once gray, drab, and postindustrial, and wild and green and timelessly Celtic. Pretty soon we were outside town and driving through picture-book rolling fields and hedgerows under very blue skies with lazy, whipped cream clouds.

Dehan was staring this way and that with slightly narrowed eyes, her aviators perched on top of her head. She said, suddenly, "Somebody shrunk New England."

I smiled. "Your first glimpse of the world outside the USA, Dehan."

She frowned at me. "You know, if you keep calling me by my surname, you'll have to call me Stone. We'll have to call *each other* Stone. That could become confusing."

I was quiet for a bit, smiling to myself. "I won't deny," I said, "that I get a foolish kick out of calling you Mrs. Stone."

She raised an eyebrow and smiled too.

I continued, "I know people don't get it, but I figure that's their problem, not mine. Either way, and even if it seems contradictory, you will always be Dehan." I shrugged. "That's just who you are to me."

"It is contradictory, but that's cool. How long is this drive?"

"Six or seven hours, through some of the most remote, beautiful landscapes this side of the Atlantic. That gets us to John o'Groats . . ."

"John o'Groats. That is some name."

"The most northerly part of Great Britain. Midsummer they get only a couple of hours of darkness at night. From there we drive west for four miles to the ferry at Gills, and from there . . ."

"The ferry to the island of Gordon's Swona, another eight miles by sea. And from there, another mile by road to the castle. So total . . . ?"

"Maybe nine hours. We should arrive at teatime."

"Teatime?"

I grinned. "It's a great institution: tuna and cucumber sandwiches cut into bite-size triangles, biscuits, rich fruitcake . . ."

"And tea."

"And tea. It tastes different when they make it here."

She was quiet for a moment, watching me. "You ever going to tell me what your connection is with this place?"

"Yup."

She waited, watching me. Finally she said, "Stone . . . ?"

"While we're here, I promise." Before she could answer, I changed the subject. "But you know what? I never heard of Castle Gordon. How did you find it?"

She shrugged and spread her hands. "I'm a detective. I detect. It's what I do."

"What did you google?"

"Whiskey, remote, castle."

"So naturally you wound up with a list of remote Scottish castles converted to hotels."

"This one was the remotest of the lot. It's only been a hotel for the last couple of years, though the Gordon family bought it back in 1980."

I glanced at her, curious. "Bought it back?"

She shifted in her seat, with her back half against the door. "Yeah, it was bought by an American with Scottish roots. His family were from the area and his ancestors owned, and then lost, the castle. His family made a lot of money during the Civil War and the drive west, and he made even more during the sixties and seventies, then moved here in the early eighties and bought the castle, which he claimed had belonged to his great-great-whatevers. The place is now run by his grandson, Charles Gordon Jr."

I was quiet for a bit, enjoying the landscape and the fresh summer breeze gently battering me through the window. After a moment I said, half to myself, "Great-great-whatevers. I remember a restaurant in Colorado that specialized in those. They called them Colorado oysters."

"Funny guy. So how long were you here, Stone? And where and when?"

"I was in London, for eighteen months, about fifteen years ago. It was supposed to be six months as part of an exchange program between the NYPD and Scotland Yard. I was in my early thirties. They kept telling me to go back to New York, and I kept finding ways to extend my stay for another six months."

"Huh." She was pensive for a moment, suspecting she already knew the answer to the question she hadn't asked yet. "What made you want to stay?"

I shrugged. "I was enjoying myself. I made some good friends . . ."

She interrupted, "And you were in love."

I nodded. "Yeah, I was in love. But that was fifteen years ago."

"What happened?"

I made a face that told her to stop asking questions and said,

"What happened? Fifteen years went by, I met a nosy, wiseass cop with a bad attitude and married her. That's what happened."

She looked away. "Fine, don't tell me."

"I'll tell you." I shrugged again. "There's not a lot to tell. There's no great secret, Dehan. I just don't want to talk about it on the first day of our honeymoon."

"I get it."

We drove on for another three or four hours, had lunch in a country pub, and finally reached Gills, at the northernmost part of Scotland, at three o'clock that afternoon. Gills turned out to be not so much a town as a loose collection of houses gathered around an intersection. There was no post office, town hall, or local store or pub that I could see. So we wound down a narrow road between rugged, green hills toward a gunmetal-gray sea, highlighted with liquid silver, that stretched out cold and deadly toward the Arctic.

We stopped on a concrete quay outside a quaint cottage with chimneys at either end that claimed to be the Ferry Terminal and climbed out to stand gazing at the misty horizon. I pointed out to sea, where large clouds were building in the far north. "Only four hundred miles, Dehan, and you're in Iceland."

She gave a small, involuntary shudder. "That's like from New York to Cleveland." She glanced up at me. "Isn't Iceland in the Arctic Circle?"

"Just outside, but you get the midnight sun there in June, and twenty-four hours of darkness in December. Here, in this part of Scotland, it gets dark about midnight, and starts getting light at about two thirty."

"I guess we went north, huh, Stone?"

I smiled. "We've still a way to go."

We crossed the bare concrete and pushed through the door into the ferry terminal. There was a man in a heavy white sweater behind a melamine counter. He looked like he'd once tried to shave but busted the razor and gave up on a hopeless task. There was the blackened, withered remains of a roll-up hanging from the corner of his mouth. He watched us come in with expressionless, pale eyes and waited for us to talk.

I essayed a smile against my better judgment and said, "We'd like to cross to Gordon's Swona . . ."

He interrupted me and said something that sounded like, "Tharteh eet poonds fer th'car, suxteen fer the missus an' suxteen fer yersen."

I narrowed my eyes, pretty sure I'd understood, nodded, and said, "That's fine."

He rang it up on his register, with small flakes of ash falling from his dead cigarette. Then he looked at me slow and steady and there was evil humor in his eyes. "Suventeh poonds."

I glanced at the register to make sure I'd understood and handed over two fifties. He took his time getting my change and handing it back. Then he leered. "Uz et the Gordon Castle yir aweetah?"

I nodded. "Yes."

"Yir ferry'll moor within the hoor, gang t'thend of yon peer an'll nay be long."

I nodded again. "Thanks."

As I turned and opened the door, he added, "Ut was plowetrery thus mornin' and a haar in from th'east thus afternoon. Tull be mochie afore the gloaming, fer-sure, an' nay doot there'll be a fair gailleann by t'morrah."

Dehan blinked furiously at him. I nodded one last time, thanked him, and returned to the car.

"What was that, Stone? Was that English?"

"With a liberal dose of Scots Gaelic. I think he said there'd be a storm tomorrow."

"You understood him?"

I didn't answer; instead I fired up the car. Fortunately the signs were in plain English and I drove to the loading point where I figured the ferry would dock, then stopped and thought for a moment.

I turned to her. "Tull be mochie afore the gloaming. It will be muggy before dusk. An' nay doot there'll be a fair gailleann by t'morrah. And no doubt there will be a fair gale, or storm, by tomorrow. Weather here is pretty unpredictable."

She stared at me for a long moment without expression. Then she said with a hint of disapproval, "You're a remarkable man, Stone."

The sea was flat and almost milky in consistency. The crossing took an hour and was unremarkable, except that the views from the deck, of the Isle of Stroma to the west and Orkney to the north, were extraordinary. There was a desolation about the beauty of the place that was not quite like anywhere else. At one point Dehan shook her head, squinting into the sea breeze, fingering her long hair from her face. "I never imagined England like this..."

I laughed. "Don't let them hear you say that. This is not England. Scotland is a country in its own right. In some ways it is closer to Scandinavia than it is to England."

She frowned and shook her head. "It's so... *remote!*"

"Yup. And you have brought us to the most remote part, of the remote part."

She took hold of my arm and squeezed it. "Good. No inspector, no Mo, no distractions, no cold cases for two long, wonderful weeks."

We stood like that for a while, enjoying the strange, peaceful desolation. It had turned warm and close, and Dehan ran her fingers over her brow. Then she gave a small laugh. "He was right!"

I smiled at her. "Hm?"

"The guy at the terminal. He said it would turn muggy in the afternoon..."

I did a fair imitation of his brogue. "Tull be mochie afore the gloaming, an' nay doot there'll be a fair gailleann by t'morrah."

She looked up into my face. "So we'll have a storm tomorrow? That means breakfast in bed and hot toddies in front of the fire."

"I'm not complaining. Bring it on."

We sighted Gordon's Swona twenty minutes later. It was a wedge-shaped island that rose dramatically out of the sea mist. The narrow end consisted of high cliffs and a relatively flat tableland towering some hundred and fifty or two hundred feet above the waves, and then sloping gently for about a mile and a half, or a little more, toward broad, rolling grasslands and white, sandy beaches. On the tableland, at the top of the cliffs, a spectacular castle stood silhouetted in the coppery afternoon light.

As we stood staring, the note of the engines changed and we began to slow, churning the water and nosing toward the beach where we could now see a small port with a long pier that had been built out of wood and concrete. Eventually, after some careful maneuvering, we eased to a halt, the apron ramp was dropped with a huge, metallic clang that threatened to take off the end of the dock, and, amid a lot of shifting, drifting, and grinding, we rolled out of the cargo hold and onto the concrete pier.

And then we stood by the car and watched as the ramp was raised, clattering and clanking, to its closed position. The ferry reversed away from the dock, turned, lumbering, and slowly took off north, toward the distant shadow of Orkney on the horizon.

Behind us, in the south, the mainland was no longer visible, but before us the road wound through gentle hills of green pasture, meadow flowers, and heather, where sheep and goats ruminated and watched us with saurian eyes, to a broad forest, perhaps a mile away, that climbed the slopes for perhaps another half mile toward the hazy silhouette of the castle on the hill. All around us, the air was rich with the smells of aromatic grasses and herbs—maybe lavender, rosemary, and thyme. It seemed very still. The only sounds were the lapping of the small waves on the shore and the lazy buzz of bees among the grass and flowers.

Ahead, about halfway up the slope, half a mile from the castle, we could just make out a small village among the woods by the road. It seemed to consist mainly of stone cottages and tall chimney stacks poking up among the trees.

I glanced at my watch. It was six o'clock, and though the light was definitely coppery and there was a feel of evening to the sultry air, the sun was still a good four hours or more from setting.

I smiled at Dehan. "Let's go."

It was a fifteen-minute drive, because though the speed limit on the island was 25 MPH, the road wended and wove in big loops, and in many parts it was rough and pitted. When we passed through the village, we saw that it consisted of a village green, a handful of houses, a two-story post office, and a picturesque pub called the Gordon Arms; and a moment later we were in the woods again, winding our way up the steep hill through tall pine trees that cast an eerie green light, until at last we broke out of the forest and onto the broad, flat, grassy tableland. There the road went straight, and ahead of us, tall and ancient, stood the castle, brooding, lowering over the dark expanse of the North Atlantic toward the Arctic Circle and the heavy, dark clouds that were gathering there.

As we drew closer, we could see that Castle Gordon was encircled by an ancient stone wall, perhaps eight feet high. But in many places that wall had crumbled over time, and where it had collapsed, leaving great gaps in the masonry, it had been replaced with hedges and trees, giving the vague impression that Nature was slowly winning in a war of attrition against Man.

The road entered the grounds of the castle through a large iron gate that stood open, and from the gate onward the road became the driveway. On either side of that drive there were well-tended lawns and formal gardens, and to the left there was a large topiary maze.

A butler in traditional dress and a page were waiting for us at the foot of the stone steps that led up to the main door. When we pulled up, the butler opened the door for Dehan and welcomed us to Gordon's Swona while the page took my keys to open the trunk, unload our luggage, and park the car. While he did that, I stood back and had a good look at the building. You could have described it as a horrific mixture of styles thrown together with a total disregard for esthetics or proportion, a monstrous affront to architecture and a grotesque stone pile. You could very well have described it like that, if you'd had no soul.

On the right-hand side, at the front, there was a massive, square, four-story solid stone tower with castellations at the top and narrow, gabled windows on the second, third, and fourth floors. On the ground floor, a leaded bay window overlooked yellow and red rosebushes, while dense ivy swarmed up the wall as far as the second floor.

The central body of the building was granite, with a gabled portico supported on ancient stone pillars, and a gabled slate roof with tall chimney pots. To my uneducated eye, it looked as though the tower was Victorian mock Elizabethan, where the main body was maybe two hundred years older, maybe seventeenth century. On the far left there was another wing in paler stone, running at right angles to the house. It was only three stories high, with small, narrow windows and battlements up top. That, I guessed, was what was left of the original castle. The overall effect was that of a messy jumble of rocks and styles, but somehow it came together and became a beautiful, ancient work of art.

"You coming?"

Dehan was standing on the granite steps smiling at me. The butler was at the door, holding it open, as though there was nothing else in the world he needed to be doing right then. The sun was bright, and the scent of the roses was strong on the air. For a moment it was a perfect, timeless scene. I smiled, said, "I'm coming," and stepped toward her, and as we climbed the steps together, a cloud moved across the sun, casting a deep shadow over the castle, and a clammy, muggy breeze touched my skin.

We stepped through the door, and the butler said, "Welcome to Castle Gordon."

TWO

WE STEPPED INTO A VAULTED, GOTHIC ENTRANCE HALL. The floor was tiled in a black-and-white checkerboard pattern, and a magnificent stone staircase rose directly in front of us, and then split in two to ascend, right and left, to a galleried first-floor landing. Immediately on our right was a reception desk, and coming out from behind it as we entered was a man in his early thirties in chinos and a blazer, with blond hair swept back from a face that was intelligent, but too kind to be handsome.

He held out a large, soft hand and smiled as we approached. "Mr. and Mrs. Stone, I imagine. How splendid that you could join us. We have a full house this summer."

There was no trace of an accent, and I figured he had been educated at an English boarding school. We shook hands and he added, as though we had asked, "Charles Gordon. My father insists on calling me Junior, because he is also Charles. So we call him Senior. He's an American, you know. Now!" He gave each of us a broad grin and held out his arms like he was about to hug us. "I imagine you will want to freshen up after a long journey. Brown will show you to your room, and we'll be having cocktails in the drawing room . . ." He gestured across the hall to a set of walnut doors. "At seven. Then you'll be able to meet our other charming guests. We'll be going in to dine at about half seven or eight."

Dehan frowned. "Half seven?" Then she grinned. "What's that, three thirty?"

Charles laughed.

I said, "Seven thirty, smart-ass. Thank you, Charles, that sounds perfect. I've heard you have an exceptional range of whiskeys."

"Second to none, old chap, and I'll guide you through them with great pleasure. I've put you in the tower, in the honeymoon suite. I trust you'll find it comfortable."

The honeymoon suite was everything you'd expect from a Hollywood rendition of a Scottish castle. There was a gigantic mahogany four-poster bed with drapes, there were gabled, leaded windows overlooking the formal gardens, a stone fireplace big enough to house a small family, and vast, bare wooden rafters overhead. The walls were oak paneled, and on the bedside table there was a silver bucket filled with ice, holding a bottle of Bollinger and two Edinburgh crystal glasses.

Once Brown had put our cases on the bed and left, Dehan stood looking around with a big smile all over the right side of her face. "Oh man," she said. "Stone."

I took off my jacket and she crossed the room to poke her head into the bathroom. "There is a freestanding tub, with clawed feet and gold taps." She turned and winked at me. "Open the champagne, big guy, we're going to have a bath, Scottish castle style . . ."

AN HOUR LATER, we joined the other guests in the drawing room.

The Gordon Castle was a boutique hotel. There was no pool, no bar, and no dining room in the usual sense of the word. More than staying at a hotel, it was like staying with a rich friend at his country manor. Instead of several hundred anonymous guests milling around a vast building in Florida, here we had just a handful of fellow guests who had cocktails in the drawing room, and lunched and dined with the family in the ancestral dining room. It was different, and it had sounded like exactly what Dehan and I needed.

The drawing room was big. The floors were wood, strewn with what looked like genuine Persian rugs, and to the right of the door as you went in, there was a huge granite fireplace. Right now there were several large logs burning in it. An eclectic collection of sofas and armchairs, standard lamps, and occasional tables were scattered around the room in an apparently random fashion that somehow managed to be homely and comfortable. Against the far wall, an elaborate credenza held an extensive collection of bottles, hand-cut decanters, and glasses. To the left of it, French windows stood open onto a stone terrace with steps down onto the lawns and the gardens.

There were a number of people standing and sitting, and they all turned to watch us come in. For a moment they looked like a bizarre frozen tableau from an early play by Agatha Christie: Charles Gordon was standing by the drinks, dressed in a tuxedo, holding a cocktail shaker. On the crimson-and-gold sofa directly in front of the fire was a woman who was still attractive in her midfifties. She had short, black hair and wore a long evening dress of deep blue satin, with a string of pearls around her neck. She had very red lipstick and regarded Dehan with wary eyes.

In an aquamarine armchair with wooden legs, also beside the fire, was another woman, blond, perhaps in her early sixties. She wore a low-cut white satin dress with a gash up to her thigh, exposing a leg that looked thirty years younger than she did.

A third woman stood by the French windows, smoking. She was younger than the other two, perhaps thirty. Her dress was mauve, and the gash, up to her hip, exposed a leg you had to try hard not to look at. She had hair that was wild, curly, and red, tied back in a mauve satin bow. Her face should have been pretty, but a spray of freckles and mischievous blue eyes made it more captivating than that.

Besides Charles, there were two other men in the room. One was standing beside the redhead. He was tall and strongly built, wearing what looked like an off-the-peg Italian suit. He had black hair and sullen eyes, which he was using to undress Dehan. I figured he was in his thirties.

The other was standing by the fire. Like Charles, he was wearing an evening suit and a bow tie. He was probably in his late fifties and had that stiff, brisk air that the British military brass all seem to acquire by osmosis.

They all smiled with varying degrees of sincerity, and Charles said in a loud voice, "Ah! You're here! Well done! Now, what will you have? Major, care to make the introductions?"

Before the major could get started, Dehan said, "Any whiskey you recommend, straight up. Stone will have the same."

The blonde in the aquamarine chair, with the low-cut white dress, turned out to be our hostess, Charles Jr.'s mother, Pamela. She smiled at me without moving, raised an eyebrow, and sipped her drink, then said, "How do you do, John?"

I caught something in her voice which I filed away under irrelevant gossip that might later be useful, and asked her how *she* did. Then the major gestured toward the woman on the sofa in the blue dress.

"Lady Jane Butterworth, Detective John Stone and his wife, Detective Carmen Stone."

She ignored Dehan but leaned forward and offered me her hand to kiss. "I don't use my title, I'm a committed socialist, you know," she said breathlessly, then laughed. "I hope you won't arrest me! Call me Bee, may I call you Stone? Such a *strong* name."

I told her I wouldn't and she could, and the major led us on to the couple at the French windows. "Dr. and Sally Cameron, very old friends of the family! Ian has his surgery opposite the pub in the village. Very handy, eh, Ian? And Sally owns the grocery store and runs the post office. Everyone does a bit of everything on Gordon's Swona, hay?"

The major laughed and the doctor looked at him with distaste. Sally stepped forward and kissed Dehan on the cheek while I shook the doctor's hand. I had seen friendlier eyes on great white sharks. We all asked each other how we did, and then the major laughed like he was telling a hilarious story and said, "And I am Major Reggie Hook, old friend of Charlie's, been coming here for years, ay, Charles?"

"Indeed!" Charles approached with two glasses of whiskey and handed them to us. With an enthusiasm that had more to do with wishful thinking than truth, he added, "We are all old friends here. Aren't we, Mummy?" Whatever Mummy was going to answer, he didn't give her a chance. He plowed on, "I think you'll like this single malt. It's from the local distillery and a bit of a hidden treasure. We have superb water here."

The thing continued in that vein for the next half hour. At first I worried that it would get on Dehan's nerves. I knew well that her tolerance of BS and small talk was limited, at best, but when I glanced at her, talking to Charles, I saw her eyes were alive and she was smiling. I also noticed Ian Cameron watching her. I didn't blame him. She was in a very simple, but very expensive black dress with no sleeves or shoulders, and a silver chain around her neck with a single amethyst. It all served to highlight her own beauty. I smiled, partly because she was mine, and partly because that very beauty hid the kick-ass, Bronx-bred bad attitude that was never very far below the surface.

Pamela stood, gave me a thin smile, and joined Dehan and her son. She gave Dehan a frigid once-over and said, "What an exquisite dress, but darling, are you in mourning? Who died?"

Dehan raised an eyebrow at her and smiled. "My tolerance for bullshit. It died a long time ago, but I'm still in mourning."

Charles burst out laughing. Dehan caught my eye, winked, and grinned.

Then the door opened, and I noticed several things all at once.

Dr. Cameron stiffened and his hostile face became even more hostile. His wife, whose side he had not left since we'd entered the room, also stiffened, but the expression on her face was anticipation, not hostility. Everybody else in the room went silent and stared, except Dehan, who caught my eye again with an unspoken question.

The man who entered the room was aware of the effect he had, and of his own magnificence. He was over six foot, but if he'd been four foot two he would not have looked any smaller. He had a powerful chest, a powerful jaw, and a mane of silver hair swept back from a large forehead. His nose was aquiline and his pale blue eyes were cruel and ruthless. He was a man born to be king in a world that no longer needed kings.

Charles moved forward. "Ah, Father, there you are. May I present Detective Carmen Stone . . ."

Charles Gordon Sr. ignored his son and moved in on Dehan like a hungry wolf moving in on an injured baby gazelle. His voice was deep and resonant, with clear traces of his Boston roots. "Detective? I'll wager most of the men you hunt down surrender willingly."

I saw the doctor turn away. Dehan shook her head. "No, most of them need a couple of slaps and their hands cuffed."

He laughed. "You make it sound so appealing."

"Yeah? The reality is a little different, Mr. Gordon. This is my husband, Detective John Stone."

He gave me the kind of look that all the women in the room were giving Dehan. There was enough acid in there right then to clean a ton of copper. He raised an eyebrow.

"Another detective? We had better all behave, then, hadn't we? Though you are, of course, outside your jurisdiction."

I stepped up and put my hand on Dehan's elbow. "*And* on our honeymoon," I added. "Thank you, by the way, for the champagne. We enjoyed it."

"Don't thank me." He said it like he meant it. "Thank my

son. And speaking of useless incompetence, Charles, am I not entitled to a drink in my own house?"

He pushed past me toward his son, who was hurrying to the drinks tray, and Pamela, Lady Jane, and Sally Cameron all seemed to be sucked into his wake, like seagulls trailing after a Spanish galleon in full sail.

"What will you have, Father?"

"Let me see . . ." He didn't so much say it as boom it. "Let me see! Shall I have something different to *what I have every single night*? Good lord, boy! Can you take the initiative on *nothing*? Not even a simple task like getting your father a drink?"

"Vodka martini it is! What a character!"

There was some simpering and giggling and I stepped out the French windows onto the terrace. The sun was low on the horizon and the evening light was turning a grainy copper. The shadows of the trees stretched long across the lawns, and above, the blue was turning dark. There was a closeness to the air, and you could almost taste the static electricity in the humid air.

Dehan came out after me and rested her ass on the ancient stone balustrade. She gave a small laugh. "We just stepped through the looking glass, but instead of winding up with Alice in Wonderland, we wound up in an Agatha Christie novel."

I smiled. "You're not far wrong." I sipped, watching her. "I hope you're not regretting it. We can move on if you want."

"Are you kidding? I love it. I never saw a group of people hate each other so politely. Is this what Brits are really like, Stone? I thought it was just the movies."

"Some. This small archipelago has a very complex society."

She held my eye a moment, still smiling. "Let's make a bet."

"What kind of bet?"

"Who will the victim be, and who will the killer be. So far I don't think it's the butler."

I laughed, then shrugged and gazed out at the slowly gathering dusk, which the Scots call the gloaming. "The victim is obvious," I said, playing her game for a moment, but feeling oddly uncomfortable about it.

"The old man? CG Sr.?" I nodded and she nodded back. "I agree."

"The murderer . . ." I shook my head. "I have some ideas, but we're here on our honeymoon, and I don't want to tempt the gods . . ."

I trailed off. It was as though the word had some hidden power of evocation. In the sky, over the broken stone wall and the trees in the north, a great plume of green light shot up into the sky, flickered, and spread out like a fan. Dehan saw my face and said, "What?"

I took her hand and pulled her to her feet, then turned her around. A violet arch swelled like a great dome from the horizon, then shimmered and seemed to break up and spread like mist. Next thing the sky had turned green, and long, vertical columns of light, like immensely tall ghosts, sprang up and wavered this way and that. From the center, a plume of red expanded, and within it, light flashed and seemed to move around in some crazy kind of dance. Dehan had gone rigid, gripping my hand as though she were trying to crush the bones. The red plume swelled, rising above the green light until half the sky was awash with eerie, alien light, twisting and flickering like a gossamer curtain over a parallel world of Norse gods and daemons. Then, as quickly as it had appeared, it began to fade.

She turned to face me. Her eyes were huge and bright. She tried to speak, but words cannot express the way you feel the first time you see the Northern Lights. So she expressed it to me a different way.

A footfall behind me made me turn. Dr. Ian Cameron stood framed in the doorway. He studied me a moment and said, "I'm sorry to interrupt. We're going in to dinner, if you'd like to join us."

Like the honeymoon suite, the dining room was exactly what you would have expected from a Hollywood production of

Murder at Castle Gordon. The ceiling was high; the table was long, dark, highly polished, and mahogany, and set with place mats because tablecloths are considered vulgar. Three large silver candelabras were set down the center, and a vast crystal chandelier made tiny rainbows of the candlelight above the table.

Charles Gordon Sr., naturally, sat at the head. Bee—Lady Jane —sat on his right and Sally Cameron on his left. I was next to Bee, with the major opposite me and Pamela on my right, with her son, Gordon Jr., on her right. Dehan was between the major and Ian.

A door opened at the far end of the room and Brown, very dignified in tails, entered carrying a very large tray with a silver soup tureen. Behind him were two girls in uniform with white aprons. They each carried a silver ice bucket with a bottle of white wine in it. I caught Dehan's eye and winked at her. While the butler was serving the soup, and the maids were pouring the wine, Gordon Sr. boomed down the table, "I am an American, Carmen."

She glanced at him. "Boston born and bred, I'd say."

He laughed like a caricature of Orson Wells at his most hammy. "See! She *is* a detective!"

"I just know my accents, Mr. Gordon. Here I'm not a detective. I am a newlywed bride."

His face went sour. "How charming," he said. "I am an American, but this island belonged to my ancestors, along with much of the coast, for at least a thousand years. It was my father who reclaimed it, back in 1980. He was obsessed with his Scottish roots. He used to wear a kilt, you know? I haven't the legs for it."

He sipped his wine and smiled at Sally. She looked away and Bee simpered. "Nonsense, Charles. You have a well-turned leg!"

"How would you know, Bee?" It was Pamela.

Bee affected to think, with her finger on her cheek. "Well, I'm blessed if I know, darling! But am I wrong?"

Everybody laughed except Pamela.

I said, "Have you been here since the eighties, Mr. Gordon?"

"Yes. Since my father, Richard Gordon, died." He stared at me, as though challenging me to ask. I didn't, so he went on, "He committed suicide in his study, almost forty years ago."

"I'm sorry to hear that."

Pamela replied, breaking a hot bread roll. "Not everybody thought it was suicide."

He snapped, "That's quite enough of that, Pamela!"

She ignored him and went on, "Some people thought it was murder."

THREE

By the end of the soup, Gordon Sr., Bee, and Sally had fallen into conversation with each other. I couldn't help feeling grateful. Ian and Pam maintained their characteristic sullen silence throughout, and Dehan, the major, and I fell into conversation about the history of the island.

"It was," the major said, "for a long time merely a glorified pig farm! Hence the name Swona. It derives from 'swine.' Keeping them on an island was safer than a farm, easier to protect and impossible for the animals to stray."

Dehan asked, "How old is the castle?"

"There has been a small fortress here since the Vikings, first intended to fend them off, and then used by them to protect their settlements. The swine were a highly prized asset, as you can imagine."

We had been served lamb cutlets with new potatoes, Vichy carrots and fresh garden peas, all from the castle's own orchards. Dehan was engrossed in her food but looked up to ask, "So when did it come into the possession of the Gordons?"

"Oh." He sipped his claret and smacked his lips. "The earliest record of a Gordon owning the island dates back to the thirteenth century. In the parish record it is stated that it was a dispute settled by contest of arms, which was won by one Charles Gordon, who fatally wounded his opponent with a blow to the head, thus rendering the estate his in lieu of monies due."

"They didn't mess around in those days, huh, Major?"

"Quite so. It remained then in the Gordon family for almost seven hundred years, until the eighteenth century, when they were overtaken by several misfortunes, not least an attack of swine fever, which wiped out the pigs on the island and ruined the family. Charles Sr.'s great-grandfather, six times over, if you follow me, sold what little possessions he had left and sailed for Boston in 1780 or thereabouts, but it wasn't until the great drive east, after the Civil War, that Charles, Richard Gordon, began to amass his fortune. He never left Boston, but he invested in cattle farms, mining, gun trafficking . . . you name it! And by the turn of the century, he was one of the richest men in Boston."

We had finished our main course, except for Dehan, who was picking up the bones and nibbling at them. She caught a glance from Pam and said, "It's finger food, right?"

Pam looked away and Brown and the maids started clearing the table. Ian got to his feet and spoke loudly over Gordon Sr.'s conversation, forcing him and Sally and Bee to turn and look. His accent seemed to have grown stronger with the wine.

"Ut's late. We need ta be gone. C'mon, Sally, git yer thungs."

Sally turned to him with narrowed eyes.

Gordon Sr. boomed, "You have not even finished your meal, man! Can't you at least wait for coffee?"

Ian's face hardened. "No. We're gone now. But thanks for a wonderful evening, *Charles!*"

Just for a moment I saw savagery and hatred in his face. Sally sighed, stood, and flounced out of the room. Ian looked at us all as though he knew some shocking truth about us and said, "I'll wish yiz all a good evening!" Then he left, trailing his self-conscious dignity.

After he had gone, Pam stood too. "Actually, I'm quite tired myself. I think I'll turn in." She did something with her mouth that could not be bothered to be a smile and added, "Night, all," and followed Ian out of the room.

Gordon Sr. heaved a big sigh and threw his napkin on the table. "Fine!" he said gracelessly. "If there is to be no entertainment, and my wife is not to attend me, then I too shall bid you all a good night and retire." He stood and stared at Dehan. "I breakfast and lunch in my chambers, but I shall no doubt see you at dinner tomorrow. Unless of course you care to pay me a visit." He paused deliberately for a long second, then turned to me, as though pretending to include me in the invitation.

I held his eye. "Good night, Mr. Gordon."

Unlike Ian, he gathered his dignity about him like robes of office and left the room.

Charles Gordon Jr. expostulated breathlessly, "Well!" Then he stammered, "We, we, um, we're left with our cozy little group then! And, and, and . . . *that's* nice! Who's for sticky toffee pudding?"

We had sticky toffee pudding, which was astonishingly good, and then withdrew to the withdrawing room to have coffee and whiskey, though Bee had cognac. We settled ourselves by the fire, the major, Dehan, and myself, armed with generous measures of single malt, while Charles and Bee took their drinks to a small card table near the French windows and played canasta together.

The major smiled happily, sipped, smacked his lips, and sighed. I looked at Dehan. She was examining her drink, and I was wondering how long it would take her to ask. It didn't take long. She raised her eyes to the major and said, "What did Mrs. Gordon mean when she said some people thought Richard Gordon had been murdered?"

He gave a small, comfortable chuckle. "Couldn't resist it, hey? Well, it was all rather peculiar, to tell the truth. Long time ago now, 1981, I suppose. Old Man Gordon, that's Charles Jr.'s grandfather, hadn't long bought the castle. His family were very rich, of course, having made their fortune in the previous century. But his passion, as I told you before, was to return to his roots and reclaim the land that he felt belonged to him and his family by right. When his wife died . . ." He paused, frowning at the fire, and mumbled half to himself, "Never really sure actually if she died or they divorced, but that's neither here nor there, really . . ." He looked back at Dehan and raised his eyebrows. "That's exactly what he did."

I sipped. "So he bought it in 1980."

"That's right. Of course, Charles Sr. was only in his early twenties at the time, finishing at university in Boston. He read law, or as you would say, he majored in law, and came out to join his father when he graduated, which must have been '81 or '82, I suppose. And what he found was a rather peculiar setup."

Dehan arched her eyebrows. "Peculiar in what way?"

"Well, for a start, it seemed that Old Man Gordon was going a bit . . . odd! He had started researching all the families that lived on the island, looking into their family backgrounds, finding out how long they had lived here and, above all, if any of them were related to him. It became something of an obsession."

I frowned. "Aren't most people in communities like this related to each other?"

He spread his hands. "Well, exactly! But he found one family, the Armstrongs, who were in fact quite closely related, via the mother, who was in fact a Gordon. And he sort of *adopted* this family."

"Adopted them?"

He nodded down at his glass. "To the extent that he was considering putting young Robert Armstrong into his will. As you can imagine, Charles Sr., when he arrived at his new home from university in Boston, was quite alarmed at the situation. His father was talking about 'raising up' the Gordons once more and 're-empowering' them. He wanted to reunite the clan . . ." He shook his head. "All sorts of mad stuff. He had clearly lost the plot, as they say these days, and Charles was understandably worried, as he could see his family's considerable fortune being squandered on some bizarre project and, frankly, pilfered by unscrupulous people claiming to be related to him."

Dehan shifted in her seat. "So, what happened?"

The major sighed. "Well, at first not very much . . . Charles begged his father to reconsider his relationship with the Armstrongs, and to put some kind of financial cap on his so-called project, but his father wouldn't hear of it. He continued to restore the castle . . ." He waved his hand around. "Forty years ago this was largely a ruin. He restored it and refurnished it with genuine antiques. That, at least, was an investment. But his increasing closeness with young Robert Armstrong, and the vast amounts of money he was spending on him and his mother, that was cause for genuine concern." He paused, tipping his glass this way and that. "Then things got much more complicated."

I raised an eyebrow and smiled. "More?"

"Yes, because Charles Gordon Sr. fell in love."

"Let me guess," I said. "He fell in love with a girl who was of the wrong social class."

The major looked a little startled.

I smiled. "I may be an American, Major, but I lived here long enough to learn to distinguish the accents. I know a non-U accent when I hear one. Even if it's been disguised."

"Oh!" He stammered a moment. "Well, yes, that was precisely it. She was the daughter of the local publican. Very attractive young woman with a very lively personality. Had a sort of saucy wit, if you follow me. And young Charles was quite captivated by her. Absolutely head over heels."

Dehan was watching him with narrowed eyes. "This is . . ." She pointed vaguely in the direction of the dining room.

He nodded. "Pam, yes." He nodded again. "Well, as you can imagine, Old Man Gordon disapproved violently of the match. He might be sponsoring Robert Armstrong, whom many would consider inappropriate, but at least he was related to the Gordons. But this girl, however delightful she might be, was neither a Gordon nor an appropriate spouse for a Gordon!"

Dehan both frowned and smiled at the same time. "I think I know where this is going."

The major chuckled. "Don't be too quick, Detective. It isn't as simple as it seems. Nobody knows exactly what happened because Charles Sr. won't discuss it, but one version of the story goes something like this:

"Things came to a head when Old Man Gordon told Charles that if he persisted in his plans to marry Pamela, he would disinherit him and leave his entire fortune to Robert Armstrong. Charles agonized for a full week. He told Pamela he could not see her, and he spent seven days either walking the grounds or locked in his room, brooding. Finally, on the seventh day, he went and spoke to his father. They spent over an hour discussing the issue, and when Charles came out he was a different man. He was elated. He ran to the kitchen and embraced the cook and the butler *and* the maids—remember, he was an American—and then he dashed off to tell Pam his father had had a change of heart! It was as though a cloud had been lifted from his mind and he had come down to Earth to realize the error of his ways. He gave Charles his blessing to marry whomever he pleased, and he told Charles he would kill the project and contact his brokers immediately to start reinvesting in solid stocks and shares, as he had done for most of his adult life."

"That's quite a turnaround."

The major nodded. "It is. It's not unheard of, but it was dramatic. And I need hardly say, a huge relief for the entire household."

I nodded. "I can imagine. So, what happened?"

"Well." He sat forward. "That's where it began to get very strange indeed. Refill?"

He went away and came back with the decanter. He refilled our glasses and settled back in his chair.

"As I said, Charles had gone straightaway to see Pam and tell her the good news. When he'd returned a couple of hours later, he went to see his father, planning to tell him that he and Pam had set a date. He knocked on the door . . ."

Dehan interrupted. "What door?"

"Of his study, across the hall, in the tower. He knocked, but there was no reply. When he tried to open the door, he found it locked. This in itself was not unusual, he tended to lock himself in his study when he was working. But he failed to answer when Charles knocked and called to him, despite the fact that, through the window, as he had arrived back home, Charles had seen his father sitting at his desk.

"Concerned that he might be ill, he kicked at the lock several times until he broke it . . ." He paused and shook his head, gazing at the flames in the fire. "It defied belief. Old Man Gordon was sitting at his desk with a bullet wound in his right temple, and his .38 service revolver lying on the floor beside him. All the windows were locked on the inside, as had been the door."

I frowned. "He committed suicide."

The major nodded several times. "That would be the logical conclusion, and it was what the coroner concluded in the end. But the detective who conducted the initial inquiry was never satisfied. Chap from Scotland Yard, came up because of the high profile of the deceased, and because Charles was convinced from the beginning that something was wrong, and frankly, we haven't got the forensic know-how up here to deal with a complex case."

Dehan asked, "What was it that didn't satisfy them?"

"Well, you must remember that in the 1980s, forensic science was still in its infancy, but this chap, Inspector Henry Green, he thought that the angle of the shot was all wrong. If you shoot yourself in the head, the entry wound should be horizontal, and there should be a great deal of scorching because the muzzle is actually touching the head. But in this case, though his prints were all over the gun, the entry wound was at a slight, forty-five-degree angle, and there was no scorching, as though he had held the gun at a distance, and at the height of his hip, which would clearly be impossible. There was also the issue of gunshot residue."

"What about it?"

"There was none on his hand."

I frowned and studied my whiskey for a moment. "So the inference was that he had been shot from a sitting or squatting position, at a distance."

"That's right, but it was clearly impossible because, as I say, the windows were all locked from the inside, as was the door. Charles, as I said, had had to smash the lock when he went in."

Dehan looked at me, frowning and smiling at the same time. "Son of a gun!" She looked back at the major. "And the cops confirmed that the door had been locked . . ."

"Oh yes, you could see very clearly where the latch had burst through the wood."

I said, "You were there?"

He nodded. "I was a friend of the family at the time, part-time PA to Old Man Gordon. There was no question but that the door had been locked from the inside."

I smiled. "Secret passages? Secret doors . . . ?"

"Not uncommon in these old castles, at all. But the police searched high and low and there was nothing. Two walls give onto the outside, a third onto the entrance hall, and the fourth gives onto the ballroom."

Dehan gave a little laugh. "A true locked-room mystery, whadd'ya know?" Then she laughed out loud. "This isn't something you lay on especially for American detective guests?"

He chuckled. "A police variation on the Canterville Ghost! No, no! I'm afraid not. That is exactly how it happened. You can read it in the John o'Groats local papers. It also made the national press, briefly. You can probably find the papers in the library." He pointed behind him at a door in the paneled wall. "Through that door."

Dehan grinned. "I might have a look tomorrow."

I raised an eyebrow at her, then smiled at the major. "We run a cold-cases unit in New York. We specialize in unsolved homicides." I looked back at Dehan, who was still grinning. "But we're supposed to be on honeymoon, remember?"

The major laughed. "Oh dear! I should have kept quiet, shouldn't I?" Then he shrugged. "But of course, strictly, this is *not* a cold case. It was closed, as a suicide."

Dehan made a face. "And that's probably what it was. The absence of GSR and burns may have a perfectly simple explanation. Easier to explain that than how the killer got out of a locked room."

"And an explanation," I said, setting down my glass, "that *we* are not going to provide." I stood. "Come along, Mrs. Stone. I am dead beat."

And we went up, arm in arm, to our ancient, Scottish bedchamber.

FOUR

WE ROSE EARLY. IT'S HARD NOT TO WHEN THE SKY
starts lighting up at 2 a.m. Dehan luxuriated in her freestanding
bath with clawed feet while I showered, shaved, and dressed. She
wasn't done by the time I'd finished, so I went down while she
soaked.

I found Brown in the hall, and he told me breakfast was served
in the dining room, and when I went in, the sideboard was set
with coffee and tea, and hot plates loaded with everything you'd
expect of a British breakfast: bacon, eggs—scrambled, fried, and
poached—kidneys, mushrooms, fried tomatoes, and pork
sausages, plus bread and an electric toaster.

I helped myself to some bacon and eggs and some coffee and
was sitting down to eat when Charles bustled in.

"Ah! Excellent! Good morning!" He gestured at the sideboard
with both hands. "I see you found your way to the grub! An
Englishman is never served at breakfast! That is true," he added as
he piled food on his plate, "of all Britons, not just Englishmen.
Not true, on the other hand, when we go abroad. When in Rome,
what!" He sat and didn't so much start eating as tackle his breakfast. "What are your plans for today?"

I sipped my coffee. "Not a lot. Take a walk, explore the island, maybe have lunch at the inn in the village."

"Excellent plan. The grouse is good, as is the duck, though technically not in season." He laughed. "They claim to have it frozen, but it tastes awfully fresh."

We ate in silence for a moment. Then he dabbed his mouth with his napkin, took his cup of tea, and sat back. "I couldn't help overhearing the major last night, filling you in on our little mystery."

I nodded. "I hope you don't mind. Dehan—Carmen, my wife —was curious. We work cold cases back in New York, so it tickled her curiosity."

"Not at all. My father always swore Grandfather had been murdered, and the chap from Scotland Yard . . . um . . ."

"Inspector Henry Green."

He glanced at me. "Yes, how clever of you to remember."

"I knew him."

"Good lord! What a coincidence!"

I shrugged. "Not really. I was there for a year and a half. We did a kind of exchange program. While you guys were trying to make your policing methods more American, Giuliani was trying to make New York policing more British." I smiled. "Our crime stats went down and yours went up. I spent some time at Scotland Yard. They moved me around a couple of times and I got to know a few people. Henry was one of them. He was a good detective. Very intuitive, but he always followed up with sound methodology."

He was staring at me with wide eyes. "How fascinating," he said, then blinked. "Well, he was inclined to agree with Father, that there had been foul play. But realistically . . ." He shook his head. "It was simply impossible that there was anybody else in the room with him."

I smiled. "Eliminate the impossible, my dear Watson, and whatever is left is the truth."

"Ah, quite so, Holmes! Yes indeed!"

Dehan appeared in jeans and a white T-shirt with her hair tied in a ponytail. She grabbed a slice of toast and a black coffee standing up and spoke with her mouth full. "You weady, big gumph?"

I smiled at Charles. "Big Gumph, that's me. You see why I married her."

He laughed politely. "There is, if you're in the mood for exploring, a rather splendid stone circle over to the west, near the edge of the cliffs—do please be careful!—and magnificent views of Hoy and Flotta, the islands, you know."

Dehan drained her cup. "Sounds just about perfect."

We stepped out through the French windows in the drawing room onto the ancient stone terrace. All traces of the threatened storm seemed to have disappeared, except the close, humid warmth. The sky was an intense, rich blue. There were no clouds, and swallows circled and swooped around the house like World War Two Spitfires in the Battle of Britain.

Dehan pointed and we moved down the broad steps, touched with green here and there where lichen and moss grew in the cracks between the stones, and started across the lawn toward a gap in the hedgerow that grew where the wall had crumbled, at some distant point in time.

We squeezed through the gap and found ourselves on a broad expanse of grassland that waved and swayed gently in the northerly breeze. In the distance we could see the dark blue of the ocean, hazy with morning mist, and just visible through that haze was the low, dark form of the Isle of Hoy, as Charles had said. I nodded in that direction.

"That's west. Let's go see those stones."

The grass was deep, up to our knees, and beneath it the ground was uneven, with thick clumps of moss, small rocks, and depressions. We picked our way slowly, and in the humid heat we were soon perspiring. Aside from the occasional lazy bumblebee, it was very quiet. Dehan looked down as she walked and thrust her hands in her back pockets. I had a hunch what was coming.

"Eliminate the impossible," she said, "and whatever is left is the truth."

"That's what the man said."

"So, in the case of Old Man Gordon, what's impossible is that he was murdered." She glanced at me and raised an eyebrow. "Right?"

"The trick, my dear Dehan, is to know what is impossible. You might equally argue that it is impossible for him to have committed suicide. In this case, Holmes' adage helps us naught."

She grunted. We had reached a small rise and I stopped to look at the view. It was vast. Now I could see small, dense mountains of dark cloud above the mist on the northern rim of the world. The storm had not gone away, it had merely backed up for a good charge. I inhaled a deep breath, savoring the rich smell of sweet grasses, lavender, and ozone.

Dehan turned to watch me, squinting in the bright sunlight. "So we can say, he must have been murdered because it is impossible that he shot himself at that angle, and also that he didn't get powder burns or GSR; or, it is impossible that he was murdered because there is no way that anybody could have been inside the room and left, leaving everything locked from the inside. So, it is impossible to eliminate the impossible, because *everything* is impossible."

"Precisely." I stepped down from the small mound and we kept walking.

"So, given that we have two incompatible impossibilities, which one do we eliminate?"

"Well, as I said, Little Grasshopper, in this case Holmes' adage doesn't help us. We need to do it the other way around. Here we are faced with two apparent impossibilities. So what we need to do is not eliminate the impossible, but include the possible."

That silenced her for about five minutes, during which I spotted, about three hundred yards away, the circle of standing stones. It was weird enough to send a small army of frozen ants crawling up my arms and up my back.

They stood maybe three hundred yards from the edge of the cliff. There were twelve of them, tall, maybe fourteen feet high, slender and irregular in shape, slightly pointed and smoky gray, patched here and there with dark green and black lichen. I paused to stare at them. Dehan stopped too.

"They look like twelve druids turned to stone."

"They are at least five thousand years old. Who the hell put them there, Dehan? And what for?"

"They are so remote, Stone . . ." She turned to smile at me, aware of the odd synchronicity, but unable to put it into words. "We'll never know, and even if we found out, it probably wouldn't make any sense to us. That's a true mystery." She turned back to the stones. "In a situation like that, how do you eliminate the impossible?"

I nodded. "Each one of those stones must weigh twenty or thirty tons. I wonder where they brought them from, and how."

She grinned. "You're not going to go all Mulder and Scully on my ass again, are you, Stone? It was built by aliens who used magnetic stone power." She came up to me laughing on unsteady feet and flung her arms around me. "You got some magnetic Stone power, big guy!"

We moved on, and slowly the ground leveled off and became flatter, and we began to hear an eerie moan where the breeze played among the megaliths. We moved in among them and Dehan touched them with her hands, as though she might be able to absorb their secrets somehow through her open palms.

"These are your ancestors," she said suddenly.

"I am not literally descended from stones, Dehan."

"You know what I mean." She turned to face me. "Your ancestors did this. You have an actual, physical connection with the men who made these circles. If not this particular one, another one in these islands. He knew how, he knew why and what for, and his genetic code is in your blood. That's pretty deep, Stone."

I nodded. "And Old Man Gordon felt that with a passion."

She leaned her back against the rock and slid down until she was sitting on the mossy grass. She plucked a stem of grass and examined it. "It's powerful stuff for some people: heritage, blood, land, identity. They are all tied together, and some people will kill and die for it. It has some kind of, almost . . ." She raised her eyes to look at me. "An almost mystical power. It's as strong as religion. Hell! Half the time it's tied up with religion." She pointed at the rocks around us. "This is some kind of temple, right?"

I sat next to her. The stone was warm against my back. "There is a school of thought that says that Ceres—the goddess of the harvest and fertility, possibly the oldest divinity of them all— circle, church, and kirk all have the same etymological root. It's all the same word, and the ancient Indo-European goddess of fertility, life, death, and the harvest was worshipped in circles like these."

We were quiet for a while, looking out at the misty blue sea. Then she asked, "So a man driven by such a deep, passionate love of his land, his island, his history and roots . . ." She picked another long stalk of grass and looked at it. "His son basically betrays him. Or at least he *feels* that his son has betrayed him, forced him somehow to abandon his dream of recapturing the ancient glory of the Gordons. He is wrenched, torn between his love for his son and his dream for his little island kingdom. His son leaves to tell the good news to his girl, and the old man takes his revolver and shoots himself."

She went quiet. Then, after a moment, she held out her right arm to her side, over my legs, with the hand curled awkwardly back, as though she were trying to aim a gun at herself.

"Usually," she went on, "when people try to shoot themselves in the temple, the autonomic reflex makes them move their hand at the last second, so they end up blowing off the top of their heads but they don't kill themselves at all. They just make a real bad mess. Also, the recoil is hard to control, even when you have the gun pressed up close. I'm having real trouble trying to understand why a man who takes that step, who decides to shoot himself, would hold the gun in such an awkward position."

I nodded, chewing my lip. "And in that position, the recoil would have been impossible to control, so how he hit the target is another mystery all on its own. But in any case, Dehan, the motive for suicide simply isn't there." I picked a long stalk of grass with a spear of corn at the top and beat her gently on the head with it. "This man who, according to your theory, was driven to suicide because his son insisted on marrying beneath his class, as a Gordon, was more than happy to disinherit his son and had almost adopted another boy from the village. His passion was not his son, it was this island, the castle, the village, the whole Gordon package. It is hard to imagine that man being driven to suicide because his son married the wrong side of the tracks."

"So that is two strokes against suicide."

"Dehan?"

"What?"

"What are you doing?"

She gave a girly giggle which should have been totally out of character but wasn't, rested her head on my shoulder, and said, "Ah, you know, just playing detective." Then she added in a mock French accent, "Exersahzing zee little gray cells, 'Estings!"

I fingered her hair absently while I gazed at the horizon. "It's a pretty little mystery, I'll grant you that."

"One thing would clinch it . . ."

She slid down so her head was on my lap and she was squinting up into my face. I smiled down at her and said, "The handkerchief."

She frowned. "My god, you are a freak. You do read minds."

I laughed. "It stands to reason."

"The only way he could have avoided GSR on his hand is if he'd had a handkerchief or something similar over his hand and his sleeve. Is that what you were thinking?"

"Yup. It fell off after he shot himself and was lying on the floor. It was disregarded as evidence because nobody thought it was important."

I made a face and shook my head. "I don't believe, Dehan,

there was any such handkerchief. If he wanted to avoid GSR on his hand, his only motive for that would be to frame somebody. If he was going to do *that*, he would have left a door or a window open and planted some kind of evidence. But what was done was exactly the contrary. There is no attempt to frame anybody here, unless the person being framed is Gordon. We can check the newspaper reports from the time and see if there are any crime scene photographs, but we'll find there was no handkerchief or anything of the sort. This was a murder set up to look like a suicide, not the other way around."

She sat up and got on her knees in one fluid movement. "So you *do* think it was a murder."

I nodded. "I have never had any doubt."

She spread her hands and shook her head in a silent question.

I echoed her gesture. "It was *too* impossible. It couldn't be impossible that it was *both* murder and suicide, could it? That only happens if somebody is managing the scene. And the scene was managed in such a way that, after scratching your head, you *have* to conclude it was suicide . . ."

I shrugged.

She nodded. "So it had to be murder. Totally circumstantial, Stone, but I agree with you. The suicide is the impossible." Then she frowned like she had a headache. "But . . ."

I laughed, got to my feet, and pulled her up. "Come on, this was just a little gray cells exercise, remember? What do you say we head for the village and have a traditional pub lunch?"

"I say you are a wise man, Sensei. Lead on."

FIVE

WE WERE APPROACHING THE HEDGE AND WALL THAT encircled the castle, on our way to the only road on the island, intending to follow it for the half mile down to the village and the pub, when we saw, about three or four hundred yards away, Bee, sitting on some of the wall's fallen stones, looking out at the landscape. She was wearing a flimsy white summer dress and a large, white hat with a broad blue ribbon around it. She spotted us approaching and waved, and we made our way toward her. As we drew closer she waved again and called, "Halloo! Hallo, you two! What a *glorious* morning! Where have you been? I *demand* you tell me!"

She beamed at us and Dehan laughed. "We went to the stones. What are you doing out here?"

She rolled her eyes and raised her hands in mock despair. "Oh, I simply had to get out! I couldn't take that woman for another *moment*!"

I didn't ask because I didn't really want to know. Dehan did because she did. "Which woman would that be, Bee?"

"Well, there is only one."

"There were two last night."

Bee raised a baleful eyebrow. "Oh, you mean that appalling Sally. No, she is not a guest at the castle, not, at least, in the conventional sense. I refer to Pamela."

"You two not pals, huh?"

"My dear, you have a gift for understatement. I despise the woman and she has the cheek to despise me back."

In spite of myself, I frowned and asked, "Isn't that how it normally works?"

"Oh, my dear boy, how delightfully American of you. Give me a hand down, will you, I'll walk you to the gate."

I handed her down from the rock she was sitting on and she took my arm. We began to walk, and Bee smiled at Dehan. "You chose well. My mother used to tell us, 'Only marry a man if you feel safe on his arm, otherwise he'll turn out to be queer or a sissy.' That's what they call 'gay' these days, and of course it's all the rage. But when I was young, we wanted men to be men."

I smiled and changed the subject. "You have a sister."

She smiled up at me. "Had. She died."

"I'm sorry."

"It was many years ago. Oh . . ." She paused and looked up at the sky, calculating. A warm breeze moved her dress and her hair in a sudden gust, and suddenly I could feel the storm in the air. "Oh, it must be nearly forty years ago." We started walking again. "She was engaged to Charles."

Dehan came around and took Bee's other arm. "Bee, do you mean that your sister was engaged to Charles Gordon Sr.?"

"Oh yes. Old Man Gordon was all for it, even though we weren't clan, because they'd be marrying into the aristocracy, albeit minor aristocracy. Would have been the cherry on the cake for him. The title is hereditary, you see. We've held it since we backed the Tudors against Richard. It would have given him a legitimacy he could not have dreamt of otherwise."

"So what happened?"

"Maggie, that was my sister, Lady Margaret Butterworth,

went out to Boston during his last year at university. Then she came back and he followed after he'd graduated. She was terribly in love with him. He is, after all, a rather fascinating man, isn't he?"

Dehan smiled noncommittally. "She was older than you."

"I was a mere slip of a girl back then. Barely twelve years old when they met. But even then I was aware of his intensity, the sheer power of the man. He was like his father, but more so. His father could never control him, you know." She sighed. "To Charles it was only ever a marriage of convenience. But to poor Maggie, he was the love of her life. She was besotted."

We were approaching the end of the wall. Around the corner were the gate and the driveway. Dehan was frowning and there was almost a sense of urgency to her questions.

"So when did he meet Pamela?"

"Well!" She said it as though it were self-explanatory. "Imagine! Accustomed to Boston and New York, moving to live on Gordon's Swona, he was out of his mind with boredom. He spent some time in London, but his father wanted him by his side. He wanted to infuse him with the same insane passion that *he* felt for this godforsaken lump of rock." She sighed again. "But Charles never felt it, and besides, he was a rebel at heart. I believe he would have done anything at all to defy his father. So he began to frequent the pub, where you are about to have lunch, and there he met Pam. She was the publican's daughter. She was very different back then, I can tell you!"

We had reached the corner and Bee drew to a halt.

Dehan asked, "Different in what way?"

Bee burst out laughing. "Well, for a start, she was amusing! She was a very, very naughty girl! She and Charles used to get up to all sorts of outrageous things. She was a hoot! I was really quite fond of her back then. She was just that bit older than me but quite anarchic and, honestly, my recollection of her was that she was always laughing. Always had this mischievous, outrageous twinkle in her eye. And then . . ." She spread her hands. "Then Charles, foolish, foolish Charles went and ruined everything by falling in love with her."

I was intrigued in spite of my better judgment. "How did that ruin everything if he was in love with her, and she was in love with him?"

She looked at me with big, round blue eyes. "Dear boy, she was *not* in love with him. She was just having fun. She never for a moment believed that it would *lead* anywhere. She was the publican's daughter, for heaven's sake! He, even though he was an American, was to all intents and purposes the Laird—the Lord of the Manor. She fully expected that they'd have their summer of shagging and then he'd be on his merry way. Instead of that, he proposed to her!"

I raised an eyebrow. "A fairy tale . . ."

"Precisely! And it only works in fairy tales. Suddenly this happy-go-lucky live wire was presented with the chance of becoming the *lady* of the manor. Her life was turned upside down. Of course she went for it, but all her priorities changed overnight. Suddenly she was concerned with appearances, form, manners, *behavior*!" She grunted. "By the time they were married, she had become the stuck-up old prig she is now."

I made a face and nodded. "A cautionary tale."

"Indeed."

Dehan asked, "So, if you don't mind me asking, what happened to your sister?"

She took a deep breath. "She was a frail little thing. Delicate constitution, you know. She became very depressed and died within a few months. They said she died of a broken heart. I think that's all tosh and nonsense. I believe she topped herself and Daddy hushed it up."

Dehan narrowed her eyes. "Topped herself?"

I said, "Committed suicide."

"Wow . . ."

Before she could say any more, Bee flapped her hand. "Never

had much sympathy, really. It's a harsh world, Carmen. If you're not strong you go down. That's the way it is." She grinned. "I knew he'd grow tired of Pam before very long, so I hung around in the wings and waited for him to notice me. It didn't take long." Dehan's jaw dropped and Bee started to laugh. "*That* is why Pam can't stand me. Stupid woman should be grateful I've taken him off her hands."

She patted my arm. "I shan't keep you any longer. You take your lovely wife to lunch. But take my advice, Mr. Stone, don't let that rake near her. He is insatiable!"

She turned and made her way up the drive toward the house, with a saucy swing to her hips. We watched her a moment, then Dehan took my arm and we started down the road toward the village.

"Can you believe that woman?"

"I think she's a gas. The world needs more people like that."

"You could be right. But what a setup, Stone . . ."

"I know what you were doing, Dehan."

"What?" Her face was a picture of innocence.

"You were fishing for motives."

She looked away, frowning. "No, I wasn't. Not as such."

"And you didn't find one. Bee's resentment for her sister's death, if she felt any, would have been directed entirely toward Charles, not his father. If anything, she would have felt some sympathy with his father."

"You're getting into this as much as I am, you fraud. Okay, so she has no apparent motive to kill the dad. But if the son is a rake, who's to say that was not learned behavior, or hereditary? And if the dad was as much a rake as the son, then maybe he upset somebody on the island."

I made a face that was skeptical. "You're speculating."

"Yeah, but we're not on a case, Detective Stone, and we are not going to arrest anybody, so I can speculate if I want to."

"In that case, it is possible."

We had entered among the trees, mostly tall, whispering pines that seemed to arch over the road like the nave of a cathedral. There was a soft, green light in the air and our voices acquired a muted echo. I took hold of Dehan's arm and stopped her gently. She smiled at me.

I said, "Don't make any sudden movements. Very gently turn around and look."

Through the pines I could see a glade, dense with ferns maybe three or four feet high. A shaft of sunlight was leaning in through the canopy above, and, caught in its beam, there was a stag with great, spreading antlers, motionless, watching us. It was a scene of perfect beauty and it made Dehan gasp. The quick intake of breath alarmed the stag and it turned and bolted, leaping through the ferns until it had vanished among the trees.

She didn't say anything. We walked on in silence, going ever down, deeper into the woods without speaking, until after twenty minutes or so we came upon the first house, an old stone cottage with flowerpots suspended beside the door, set back a little from the road. After that, the houses became more numerous and the woods fell back until we came to a large clearing with a green, a post office, a grocery store, and an inn.

The inn was half-timbered with a red slate roof and a tall, redbrick chimney. A sign swinging outside proclaimed that it was the Gordon Arms. We pushed open the door, a bell clanged, and the warm sound of conversation greeted us, along with the good smell of roasting meat and baking pies.

There were a few men at the bar drinking dark brown beer with no froth. I leaned on the counter and the publican, a cheerful, round-faced man in his forties, grinned at me and said, "What'll it be, sir?"

"Two pints of best, and we'd like to have lunch."

"Nay problem. Thus the dining room though thar. I'll bring yer pints to yiz."

I followed the direction he'd pointed in through an open door into a long room with a large, open fireplace and a dozen tables set with cutlery. Only one of them was occupied. It was occupied by a woman who sat staring at us. She attempted to smile, but failed.

Dehan came up beside me. "Hello, Mrs. Gordon," she said. "Are you having lunch here? Would you like to join us?"

Pamela opened her mouth, then closed it again.

"No . . . I mean, I am not having lunch. I just stepped in for a quick drink and wanted to get away from the . . ." She waved her hand at the public bar next door. Then she tried to smile again. "I'll join you for a drink, then I'll leave you to your lunch. I had better get back. Charles will be wondering . . ." She trailed off, then gestured at the chairs opposite her. "Won't you join me?"

As we sat, Dehan went straight in. With a bright smile she said, "We bumped into Bee on the way down here."

Pam sighed and looked away. "That woman!"

I said, "Have you known her long?"

"Forever!" She said it with feeling. "It feels that way, anyway."

Dehan nodded, with big innocent eyes. "Were you at school together?"

Pam laughed without humor. "Gosh, no. I went to the local comprehensive. Lady Bee went to Benenden."

Dehan frowned and shook her head. "What is that? Local comprehensive and Benenden?"

I let Pam explain. She sighed, and there was a whiff of condescension about her. "Comprehensive school. What you would call state school. And Benenden is the private girls' school that little aristocrats go to, to learn to be proper ladies."

There was no mistaking the vitriol in her voice.

"Oh." Dehan glanced at me. "I hope my question wasn't intrusive . . ."

Pam shook her head and sighed. "No, sorry, you weren't to know . . ." The barkeep came in with our pints, handed us the menu he had under his arm, and Pam said, "Bring me another G and T, would you, Len?"

"Comin' right up, Pam!"

He went away and she flopped back in her seat. "It just gets so wearing sometimes. Keeping up the pretense. I tell you, some-times I think, if I could turn the clock back and do it all again . . ."

Dehan nodded, smiling ruefully. "I hear you. I tell you." She pointed at Pam across the table. "Sister, you can get it right a million times, but you only need to fuck up once to regret it all your life."

Pam seemed to thaw. Her smile became more human. "You got that right. But you know? The biggest mistakes? The ones you will definitely regret all your life? They're the ones where you are not true to yourself. It sounds cynical, but it's true: you let somebody else down and that's bad. You'll regret that. But let yourself down and you will pay for it your whole life long!"

I made a face and nodded a lot. "That sounds like wisdom. I'll drink to that."

I raised my glass to her and pulled off a long draught while she watched me curiously.

Dehan took a long pull, then wiped her mouth on the back of her arm and looked at me wide-eyed. "Man! That is something else! This is beer?" She held up the glass in front of her face and said with feeling, "Where have you *been* all my life?"

Pam burst out laughing. I did too, but as my laughter subsided, Pam laughed more. It was as though Dehan had opened a valve with her sudden expostulation, and Pam covered her mouth with her hand and squealed a strange, half-strangled outburst. Dehan joined in, and I sat and watched them both, smiling to myself and shaking my head.

Then Dehan was leaning across the small table, gripping Pam's arms, repeating, "*This is beer? They've been lying to me all my life! Man! I just died and went to Scotland!*"

She leaned back with a foolish grin on her face, chuckling and watching Pam through hooded eyes, while Pam wiped hers and said, "Oh! I'm sorry! I don't know what came over me. I haven't laughed like that . . . I can't remember since when."

Dehan's expression changed. There was just a hint of compassion in her eyes. "Too long," she said, and then, "Say, what's so important? Join us for lunch."

After a moment, she smiled and turned to me. "Do you mind? You're on your honeymoon with this lovely lady. I don't want to intrude . . ."

"You're not intruding," I said.

Dehan added, "Please, stay, and tell us all about yourself, your castle, your life . . ."

SIX

WE DIDN'T HAVE DUCK OR PHEASANT BECAUSE THEY were not in season and it just didn't feel right, so we had steak and kidney pie instead. It was homemade and superb. So while Dehan continued with her Oscar-winning performance as a vivacious, lovable bad girl from the Bronx, soul sister to her Orkney Isles counterpart, I concentrated on my luncheon and listened. It started with an innocent question. Dehan speared a roast potato, paused, and shook her head.

"I love this place, Pam. When you work cold cases, homicides in the Bronx, this is like paradise. But I have to ask you, don't you get bored? I mean, too much paradise is like too much of anything. There are only so many times you can go and marvel at the standing stones."

Pam heaved a huge sigh. "You have no idea." She turned and gazed out the window, ignoring the food in front of her. When she next spoke, her accent had slipped slightly and there was more than a hint of her brogue trying to get through.

"Can I be really honest with you? I know this is kind of crazy, and maybe it's because I've had a couple of G and Ts already, but I feel you'll understand."

Dehan reached across the table again and covered her hand.

"Hey, Pam, a couple of weeks and we'll be gone. What you tell us stays right here, with us."

It didn't make a lot of sense, but it sounded good and it was what Pam wanted to hear. She squeezed Dehan's hand and let the gin do the talking.

"When I met Charles—I mean, I wouldn't say a word against him, he's my husband—but when I met him it was totally different. We were just having a laugh, you know? He'd come over from America for a holiday, and straightaway he'd come to the pub, sometimes he'd even have his luggage with him, you know? Like, it was on his way to the house, he had to pass by, so he'd stop. And before you knew it, we was gassing and hooting and he was a right laugh, so he was."

She paused, looking at Dehan, studying her face. When she spoke again, her expression was almost apologetic.

"I didn't talk like this back then. I had the local accent. He didn't care. He liked it. He said it was sexy. It was funny." She glanced at me, then back at Dehan. "Happy days. But be careful what you wish for, right?"

She paused again. I ate and waited.

Dehan said, "What did you wish for?"

She sighed. "The stupid thing is, I wasn't in love with him. He was a gas. He was real good fun. But I would not have dreamt in a million years of marrying him." She sat up, wide-eyed, and spread her hands. "But then the daft git went and proposed! He was a fucking millionaire, for fuck's sake! A multi-multi-multimillionaire! And I didn't even own the house I was living in! What was I supposed to do?"

She slumped back in her chair. "At first I was going to tell him no. It was crazy. It was too much. I was actually scared of what would happen, of how much things would change. But my dad got really angry with me, and some of my friends. They were all thinking, you know, how it would benefit *them*. And in the end I was weak and I kidded myself it was a dream come true. When really what it was, was the beginning of a fucking nightmare."

Dehan took a long pull on her beer and smacked her lips. "How come? I mean, I get he's a bit eccentric." She grinned. "Maybe a bit of a drama queen. But a nightmare? You're rich, you can do whatever you like, can't you?"

She shook her head. "The first thing he had me do, as soon as we were married, was change *everything* about myself: the way I dressed, the way I talked, the way I *behaved*, all my friends, I had to stop seeing my family so often. In exchange, they were shipped off to the mainland and put up in a big house with a monthly allowance, but I got to see them only once a year, in the week before Christmas. He completely isolated me and he completely erased the woman he said he had fallen in love with, to replace her with . . ." She gestured at herself. "*This!*" She shrugged. "Now, how does that make *any* sense? Why? Why did he marry me in the first place, if he wanted a different woman?"

Dehan shook her head. "People can be weird like that. Was it a power thing? Was he proving that he owned you?"

I couldn't stop myself. I said, "Was he punishing his father?"

She sighed and shrugged. "Probably all of the above. I wasn't a Gordon. We were originally from the mainland. My mum and dad came over when I was a wee baby, to run the pub. So as far as Old Man Gordon was concerned, I didn't even exist. Well, he may as well have been right, because his son set about systematically erasing me."

Dehan grunted. "That sucks, Pam. I can see why you're mad at him."

Pam snorted. "That was just the start of it. We got married just a week after his father died. It was like he couldn't wait. He went kind of crazy. And where before he was wild, after his father was killed he became kind of eccentric, you know? He became arrogant and all kind of superior, where he had never been like that before. It was as though, now that his dad was dead, he had to take over from him. He insisted I had to be the 'Laird's wife' and behave and speak appropriately. He even kind of anglicized his own accent." She paused, staring at the tabletop, ignoring her untouched food in front of her. "But the worst thing of all, after I had done all that, after all the sacrifices I had made for him, the worst thing was when he started having his affairs."

Dehan froze, like she hadn't known all along. "Oh," she said, and then, "Bee?"

Pam nodded. "Among many others. But Bee was special. It's complicated." She sighed, rubbed her eyes, and suddenly the not-quite-perfect cut glass accent was back. "I'm sorry. You don't want to hear all this. I am intruding on your honeymoon and it's unforgivable of me."

"Hey, come on. You think I didn't notice?" Dehan leaned her elbows on the table and looked her in the eye. "Us girls have to look out for each other." She glanced at me and grinned. "No offense, Stone, man. But you understand, right?"

I raised an eyebrow at her that said she was overdoing the act. "Hey, I'm just sittin' here groovin' with my pie, sista."

She told me with a wink that she didn't give a damn, she was having fun. I kept on eating and she turned back to Pam. "It was pretty damn clear last night that CG Sr. was being a pain in the ass, and you'd had enough."

Pam nodded. There was something tragic about the way she did it. "Sally is his latest. Women seem to find him fascinating for some reason. It must be the combination of his wealth, his power, and his total lack of inhibitions." She sighed, picked up her fork, and prodded her food. "He was engaged to Bee's sister, you know. She died a few months after he broke it off with her. Most of her friends and family suspected suicide, but nothing was ever proved. You'd think Bee would hate him, wouldn't you? But instead she stepped right into her sister's shoes and became his long-term lover."

Her eyes drifted toward the window and for a moment she looked as though she was going to make a move to leave again. Dehan preempted her.

"So what was the old man like? You must have known him quite well. Did you get on?"

She kept looking at the window, but she smiled. "Oddly enough, we did get on. He was all right." She blinked and turned to look at Dehan. "He was what he was. D'you know what I mean? He didn't pretend to be anything but the arrogant, ruthless, obsessed bastard that he was."

"So you did know him well?"

"Oh, aye." Her accent was slipping again. "He used to come to the inn, often on a Sunday for a Sunday roast. Part of his act as the Laird, you know, mixing with the riffraff, staying connected with 'his subjects.' I used to tease him. I was a shameless flirt back then. I'd make him laugh and more than once he bought me a drink. Aye, we got on okay.

"When his son proposed to me, he came out straight and told me. You're not right for him, and he'll not make you happy. And he was right, God bless him. I wish I'd listened."

I said, "Did you resent him for saying that?"

She shook her head. Then she hesitated and made a face. "Not at first. I agreed. But then, as everybody started pressuring me, and forcing me to change my mind, then I did, a bit."

Dehan pointed to her glass. "One for the road?"

"Ah, go on then. It's good to get all this crap off my chest, I can tell you. I've never spoken to anyone about it. You should be a fucking psychologist. I tell you, you have a gift." She smiled at me. "Hasn't she?"

"She has that, Pam. No question."

Dehan smiled. "So, come on, level with me. Your husband is convinced that his father was murdered. You hinted at that last night. So what do you really think?"

She shook her head. "Nah, that's nonsense. I was just winding him up. It is *so* typical of him, shifting the blame. *He* killed his father, with his arrogance, with his ruthlessness. The old man had a dream, let him have his dream! We could have been lovers. He was not in love with me, and I was not in love with him. We could have just had the occasional shag and let it run its course. He could have married Bee's sister, or some rich Gordon from Scotland or America, who would have suited him better. But he had to stick it to his dad, hurt him, humiliate him. And also, he wanted a woman he could control and shape and *possess*!" She shook her head. "No, he killed his dad the same way he killed Margaret. He broke their hearts, but rather than admit it and take responsibility for what he's done, he says it was murder. Who? Who would murder the old man? And what for?"

I had finished the pie. I laid down my knife and fork and drained my pint of bitter, then suggested, "A jilted lover?"

She looked surprised. Len appeared smiling at Dehan's side.

"Everything okay? Are we happy?"

I made a face of contentment. "I'm happy, Len, but you know what would make me delirious? Some Stilton cheese and the best local single malt you have."

He made a face that was conspiratorial. "Ooh," he said. "We have some fine whuskeys in the Orkneys. No doot aboot that. I've a ten-year-old Highland Park there that'll have yiz singin' your heart oot afore the afternoon's done. Ut's the northernmost distillery in the world, so it is, and one of the oldest and the finest. Started as an illegal still in Orkney by one Magnus Eunson in 1790. A priest by day and a smuggler by night, God bless his heart."

I raised an eyebrow at him. "Who do I have to kill to get some?"

He laughed. "Nerry a soul. I'll bring yiz a dram right away."

Dehan raised a hand. "Make it two." She pointed at Pam, who shook her head, and Len went away with our plates. I was wondering how I could subtly reintroduce the question without sounding as though I was prying, but Pam didn't need reminding.

"He wasn't like his son in that way. He had a lover, but he didn't cheat, he was in love with his castle, his family, his fantasy."

Len returned with a slab of Stilton, a bottle of Highland Park single malt, and two shot glasses. He winked at me. "I'll leave yiz the bottle, save mah legs havin' ta keep runnin' back an' forth!"

He left again, and Dehan poured while I helped myself to

some cheese. While I cut, I asked Pam, "Who was his lover? Was she a Gordon too?"

She shook her head. "No, I don' think so . . ."

"What happened to her?"

"I don't know . . ."

"And you? Are you from one of the clans?"

She didn't answer. Instead she said, "I mean, you'd think he'd have been concerned about interbreeding. I mean, I *know* clan is not the same as family. It's not exactly genetic, but even so, it's got to be healthy to mix, at least with other clans, don't you think?"

She had been sipping steadily at her G&T on an empty stomach, and suddenly she looked as though gin might be mixing with all the emotions Dehan was stirring up, and going to her head. But something in what she'd said made me curious.

I frowned. "Did he have plans to marry again?"

She stood suddenly. "I don't know. Look, I had better go. I think I need to lie down." She smiled at Dehan and gripped her arm. "Thank you. See you at dinner." And she walked out on unsteady legs. Dehan got up and moved around to sit facing me in the chair Pam had just vacated. She was quiet for a moment, looking out the window. I saw her narrow her eyes, I heard a car start up and move away up the hill, and then Dehan looked at me and made a face.

"You touched a nerve, partner."

I nodded. "This is damn fine whiskey and damn fine cheese."

She nodded. "Agreed." She cut a slice and sat eating it. Then she drained her glass. "Man, that is good." She refilled us both and pointed at me. "You have a theory, don't you?"

I nodded. "I have a theory that we are on our honeymoon and outside our jurisdiction."

She started a little singsong, like a schoolkid, with a silly grin on her face, holding her glass. "You have a theory, you have a theory."

"Shut up, Dehan."

"Not till you tell me your theory."

I drained my shot and cut more cheese while she refilled it. Finally I smiled.

"Fine, but it is only preliminary, okay?"

"Cool . . ."

I took a deep breath.

SEVEN

An hour later I asked Len to get us a cab to take us up to the castle and he told us Bobby had a car he sometimes used as an unofficial taxi service, there being no actual taxis on the island. We paid up, he went to make a call, and we went to wait outside. There was a wooden bench beside a couple of troughs brimming over with flowers and we sat there, feeling sleepy in the afternoon sun. It was probably only in the high sixties or low seventies, but the humidity was high, and it made the afternoon sultry and sleepy. Dehan rested her head on my shoulder and as I yawned, I noticed two people outside the post office.

It was Dr. Cameron and his wife, Sally, standing beside a new Volvo, having what was turning from a heated conversation in harsh whispers to an out-and-out row. Suddenly she turned away from him, moved to the back of her car, and opened the trunk, obscuring him from my view. Then she marched into the grocery store beside the post office and I heard him shout, "Don't you walk away from me when I'm talking to you!"

He came into view moving toward the door just as Sally emerged again, carrying two boxes, one on top of the other, loaded with groceries. He spoke to her savagely, but too quiet to hear what he was saying. She ignored him and put the stuff in the trunk, then turned and went back into the shop. He went after her, and I wondered whether I should go over and make sure she was okay. But a few seconds later, she reemerged carrying four plastic bags filled with more groceries, with him still trailing behind her, still speaking savagely, but now stabbing the air with his finger for emphasis, even though she couldn't see him.

She dumped the stuff in the trunk and closed it, then turned to face him. She cut him dead and spoke loud enough for me to hear.

"Leave me alone, Ian! Maybe ten, maybe eleven, maybe tomorrow. The answer is, I don't know! Do you understand that? *Can* you understand that? I-don't-know! Now leave me *alone!*"

She walked around the car to the driver's side and opened the door. He went after her at a run, pulling at her shoulder, speaking louder now, "Ye can't do this! It's wrong, fer God's sake! *Sally!*"

She spun and her face was flushed. She half yelled at him, "*Leave me alone, Ian! Or so help me God, I'll . . .*"

She didn't finish telling him what she'd do. She climbed in the car and drove away at speed, toward the castle. He shouted after her, but she couldn't have heard him. After that, he turned and stormed into the post office, slamming the door behind him.

A moment later an old Ford Mondeo rolled up and a man in his fifties with a face like a granite cliff and eyes like a couple of icebergs climbed out and looked at me. "Yous the Americans gone up't Castle?"

I said, "Yup," and gave Dehan a shake.

She sat up yawning and we climbed in the back, where she crawled under my arm and said, "Wake me when we get there."

I saw him glance in the mirror as he slammed the door.

"I'll no take ye past the gate."

I frowned. "Why not?"

He pulled away and we moved at a sedate twenty miles an hour up through the woods. I saw his eyes in the rearview mirror. "Tha' there castle, friend? By rights tha' should be mine. But tha' bastard—excuse mah language in front o' yer missus—tha' *bastard* Gordon stole it from uz."

I was surprised. "Charles Gordon stole that castle from you?"

"Ay, tha' he dud."

"I thought his father bought it."

He nodded, still watching me in the glass as we moved slowly through the tunnel of whispering pines. "Aye, he dud. But while his son were away in America, I . . ." He tapped his chest with his finger. "*I* was here, helpin' the old man fix the place. An' he says ta' me, 'Bobby, yer moore like a bairn to me than my own boy,' so he did. I were wi' him every day, workin' talkin' plannin', *dreaming*! He were an American, but his blood was Scottish, more'n many I ken. An' he promised me tha' castle. He said, 'Bobby, when I die, thus castle is fer thee. Fer thee's more mah bairn than mah own kith and blood.' God is mah witness. So I'll no go into those grounds until ut's to claim it as mah own, see?"

I made a face and nodded. "I understand, the gate will be fine." I thought for a moment and then said, "So you must be Robert Armstrong."

"Aye."

"I believe the old man had a great deal of affection for you and your family. You are related to the Gordon clan, is that right?"

"Aye, tha's correct. On mah mother's side. Mah father, God rest his soul, was an Armstrong, James Armstrong. A good man till he died. An' after he died, we had a fierce struggle t' survive . . ." He nodded toward the castle that had just come into view across the flat expanse of grassland. "Until Old Man Gordon come along, an' promised to take care of uz. Then we had hope, so we did, fer a while. Till his bastard son come back from America."

I scratched my chin. "Did you ever consider contesting the will?"

"Nah. 'S'what my gerl-friend says to uz. 'Bobby, why din'ya contest the will? Yiz would'a got something!' But how would I know aboot contesting a will? I ask you! Ah know aboot building, an' gardening, workin' the land, honest labor! Ah don't know about lawyers and their feckin' lies."

"I can see why you're mad."

He glanced in the mirror again and an expression you could only describe as evil cunning seemed to crawl over his face. "But mah gerl-friend, Lizzie, see? Now, she's workin' as a secatery fer a firm o' lawyers over on the mainland, and she knows aboot wills. So maybe the old bastard might get a surprise yet, so he might!"

He came to a halt outside the gates. I woke Dehan and we climbed out. I paid Bobby Armstrong his money while she yawned and stretched, and he turned around and drove away, toward the woodlands. The sky behind the castle had turned dark with cloud, and I found I was perspiring under my jacket. I grabbed Dehan and we started to walk down the long drive toward the great pile of stone and the storm which was brewing behind it. I said, "I need a shower and an hour's sleep. How about you?"

"Nope. I need an hour's sleep and a shower."

"That dovetails nicely, then."

As we approached, to the right of the great tower and a little bit beyond it I spotted Sally Cameron's Volvo parked beside the kitchen orchard, outside what I now realized were the steps that led down to the kitchen. When we reached the main entrance, I had a thought and said to Dehan, "You go on up. There's something I have to do. I'll join you in a minute."

She gave me a sleepy frown. "What are you up to, Stone?"

I shrugged. "Maybe nothing. I'll be up in five minutes."

She climbed the steps and pushed through the door while I went around the side of the tower, where Sally Cameron's Volvo was parked. Just beyond the steps that led down to the kitchen, there was a door that seemed to be a storeroom of some sort. I descended the stairs, tapped on the door, and opened it.

I found myself in a large, old-fashioned kitchen, with a heavy oak table in the middle, an ancient iron range, and cupboards that might have looked new in the 1920s. There were also a number of people there, and they were all staring at me with startled faces.

There was Brown, the butler, dressed as though he belonged with the cupboards, there were two pretty young girls in maids' uniforms, one a redhead and the other with very black hair and very blue eyes, and there was a woman in her fifties dressed in jeans and a sweatshirt that claimed to be from UCLA. She had been rolling pastry on the table and had stopped in mid-roll to scowl at me.

It was the butler who spoke. "Good afternoon, sir. Would you be lost at all?"

I smiled. "No. I thought I recognized Mrs. Cameron's car."

He nodded. "Aye, she's only after delivering the groceries."

The cute maids grinned at each other and started giggling. The redhead looked at me with a dangerous smile and said, "Och, aye, and noo she's delivering som'at else!"

Cook scowled at her and snapped, "Peggy! Mind yer tongue!"

Peggy had no intention of minding either her tongue or her business. Her white cheeks flushed red, and she stared at Cook with bright, insolent green eyes and said, "Am I lying? Is it a lie? Is she no upstairs delivering som'at else?"

I decided I liked Peggy, but Cook clearly didn't agree. She stared at the butler with furious "do something about this child" eyes and said, "Mr. *Brown!*"

Mr. Brown made a face of reproof at the girls and snapped, "You two! Off with yous. Go and polish the silver fer tonight, and keep your mouths shut!"

They flounced off prettily and within seconds started giggling again. I said, "I'm sorry, I seem to have . . ."

"Och, not at all, sir. Mrs. Cameron is upstairs, sir, um . . . delivering . . . uh . . . attending to . . ."

I raised my eyebrows and smiled. "Perhaps the verb is unimportant," I said. "I'll settle for the location."

He smiled a little sickly and muttered, "Mr. Gordon Sr., sir. A private matter . . ."

"Of course, well, it wasn't anything vital. Perhaps I'll catch her later."

"Indeed, sir."

I left the way I had come and made my way up to our room deep in thought. When I went in, I saw Dehan had thrown the covers off and was lying under a single sheet, fast asleep. The window was open, but it was still close and warm. I went into the bathroom, stripped, and had a long shower, hot, cold, hot, and then cold again. By the time I had dried myself off, the food and whiskey-induced fogginess had cleared. I pulled on a pair of jeans and sat by the window for a while, looking out at the gardens and thinking.

It was almost forty years ago, but to this small group of people it was like it had happened yesterday. All the passions, the relationships, the motives . . . They were all as alive and real today as they had been back then. And Dehan had sensed it, that was why she hadn't been able to leave it alone. And it was why I felt the same.

Eventually I pulled on some socks and boots and a shirt and made my way down again to the drawing room. There was nobody there, so I crossed the room and tried the library door. It was open.

The room was large. Maybe forty or fifty feet square with dark bookshelves rising fourteen or fifteen feet to the ceiling. The windows were leaded and the light that came through them was dappled by leaves. There were a couple of writing desks and a nest of Chesterfields around a cold fireplace. A long, dark map table occupied the middle of the floor.

It took me about ten minutes to locate the big leather-bound books that held the old newspapers. Ten minutes after that, I began to find the articles reporting Old Man Gordon's death. There were a number of photographs. He had been a very handsome man, with intense, penetrating eyes. It's hard to tell from a photograph, but I thought he had the eyes of a fanatic. Some of the articles gave potted biographies and I noted with a mixture of irony and interest that the old man's wife, Gordon Sr.'s mother, had not been Scottish.

There were a couple of grainy pictures of the crime scene too. I wasn't surprised to find that there was no handkerchief on the floor. You don't lock yourself in a room to blow your own brains out, and then cover your hand to avoid GSR.

Henry Green had been right. The old man had been murdered. By whom was not so hard to answer. The pool of suspects was pretty small, though the obvious candidates were not necessarily the right ones. How was the real challenge.

How do you get into a locked room, shoot somebody in the head, plant their prints on the weapon, and then leave, without unlocking the door or the windows, and with no secret passages?

I read carefully through all the reports but they didn't add anything new to what I already had. In fact, I had a bit more than the reports had. I had at least one motive nobody seemed to know about.

I got up and made my way back to the drawing room. Charles Jr. was there having coffee with the major. They looked surprised when I came in. Charles smiled.

"Ah, you've been exploring the library. Splendid! It really doesn't get enough use. Did you find anything you liked? Have some coffee."

I told him I would and sat in a chair by the fireplace. Outside, the light had dimmed and the breeze was turning into a blustery wind. He rang the bell for Brown and I said, "I was looking at the newspapers, the articles on your grandfather's death. I hope you don't mind."

He laughed. "Our pet mystery. No, not at all. I doubt it will ever be resolved. If it *is* even a mystery at all. I suspect he'd just gone completely batty and shot himself."

I shrugged. "You may be right, but if it had been my case, I wouldn't have closed it. I think Henry was right to be uncomfortable. The absence of gunshot residue on his hand is very troubling. It is not possible to discharge a weapon, especially in a closed room like that, and not get GSR on your hand. The angle of the shot, also, is really, to be honest, not possible."

They were both staring at me fixedly. Finally, Charles said, "Good lord, you're quite serious."

The major muttered, "My word . . ."

I laughed. "By all means, tell me to butt out. I'm supposed to be on honeymoon, and this isn't even my continent, let alone my jurisdiction, but I guess it's just professional habit. If I were back home, I'd be telling my inspector that this was a homicide that should be reopened."

Charles Jr. stammered for a moment, then said, "Well what do you suggest I should do? The case was closed and the coroner ruled it a suicide. I'm not sure one can just . . ."

The door opened and Brown came in with more coffee on a tray. He poured me a cup and handed it to me, then withdrew.

I sipped. "That's your call, Charles. Maybe it's something you should discuss with your family. There's probably nothing you *can* do without fresh evidence anyway. I'll tell you what, though: would you object to my having a look at the room where it happened? I have to admit, this is like a red cloak to a bull for me. I can see as clear as day that it could not have been suicide, but I'll be damned if I can see how it was done." He stared at me and I raised a hand. "Forgive me if I am insensitive."

"No! No, no! Not at all! I wasn't even born at the time. Um, I'm not sure how Daddy would feel, or Mummy for that matter, but I suppose they needn't know, need they?"

He grinned at the major, who beamed and said, "Top hole!"

EIGHT

AT JUST BEFORE FOUR O'CLOCK, DEHAN HAD WOKEN UP to find I was not there.

She rose, went to the bathroom, and showered, then pulled on some jeans and a sweatshirt and went downstairs. She found the entrance hall empty and silent and went to the drawing room expecting to find everybody having afternoon tea. But the drawing room was empty too, though the French windows were open and a breeze that was turning into a blustery wind carried snatches of loud conversation across the lawn to her. She stepped over and looked out.

She saw Bee sitting at a white, wrought iron table on the terrace some thirty or forty feet away. Her dress was flapping in the rising wind and she held her hat down on her head with her left hand. She was looking up at Pamela, who was standing, leaning forward slightly, with her back to Dehan, her fists clenched by her side. Dehan had been about to step out, but something about their demeanor made her pause and withdraw a little back into the drawing room.

Bee was saying, "My dear Pamela, if he upsets you so much, why don't you simply divorce him?"

Pam's voice was shrill, and Dehan wondered if she had

continued drinking after she'd left them at the pub. She spat her words at Bee like venom. "And leave him all for you? You'd like that, wouldn't you!"

Bee's laugh was a shrill hoot. "Oh, Pam! You must be drunk! What utter nonsense! After all these years? Don't be so absurd!"

"*Don't patronize me!*"

"Then don't be such a child! You've been married almost forty years! And you *still* get upset! It's too foolish of you."

Pam took a step toward her, pointing back toward the French windows. Her voice was savage. "I have given the best years of my life . . . no . . . *all my life!* to that . . . that *parasite*! And he treats me like . . ."

"Pam, darling, he treats you like what you are: a foolish child who after a lifetime of marriage has still not grown up!"

"*How dare you!*"

Bee looked away and sighed. "Oh, do stop dramatizing everything. What did you expect?"

"I expected my husband to love me! I expected at the very least to be respected! *I did not expect to be humiliated and insulted every day for the rest of my life!*"

Bee turned back to face her and there was something sad, almost compassionate in her expression. She sighed and said simply, "Oh, Pam . . ."

Pam pointed a trembling finger at her. "Don't you *dare* patronize me!"

"Oh, do stop, darling . . ."

"How you can . . . !"

Bee's voice was suddenly animated. "How *I* can? My dear girl! How *you* can, after all these years *married* to the man! Why, you must surely have realized what he was like by now! How can you *still* be shocked by his behavior?"

Pam's hands went to her face, her shoulders hunched, and she started to sob. Her voice came twisted and damp with tears. "But that . . . that *awful* woman! Why? How can you *stand* it, Bee?"

Bee sighed again, but this time with weariness. "What choice have I got, Pam?"

"You could leave him! We should both leave him!"

Bee gave a small laugh. "No, I couldn't. He knows we won't." She paused, watching Pam sob. After a moment she said, "The difference between us, Pam, is that you never loved him. I have always loved him, not in spite of what he's like, but because of what he is like. He is a beast, an arrogant, bad man, and I adore that in him. But you, you simply grew to need him. And the more he ill-treats and humiliates you, the more you need him. You should leave him. Really you should. You should teach him a lesson."

Suddenly Pam's voice was shrill. "*Oh, I will! Believe me, I will!*"

She turned and rushed toward the French windows. Dehan stepped out and Pam almost collided with her. As she pushed past, she stopped and stared at Dehan, her face streaked with mascara and tears.

"No doubt it will be your turn next!"

And next thing, she was rushing across the drawing room toward the door. Dehan looked at Bee, who still sat at the table, holding down her hat against the wind. Dehan fingered her hair from her face and approached. Bee looked away.

"This wind!" she said. "I should go inside, but I rather like it. It blows the cobwebs from one's mind."

Dehan sat. "Pam looked pretty upset."

For a moment it was as though Bee hadn't heard her, then she said, "You'd best ignore her. Enjoy your honeymoon. Don't get involved."

Dehan narrowed her eyes and chewed her lip a moment. "It's hard to ignore something like that." After a moment she added, "My father told me once that if people invested as much effort in not ignoring things as they do in ignoring them, the world would be a nice place to live in."

Bee smiled. "You Americans are forever telling stories about what your fathers 'always used to say' to you. I wonder if any of them are true."

"That one is. He was a great one for not ignoring things. I'm the same."

Bee raised an eyebrow at her. "Is this the same relentless persistence you use when interrogating your suspects?"

Dehan shook her head and smiled. "No. Usually I take them down a back alley and beat seven bales of shit out of them."

Bee threw back her head and hooted with laughter. "Oh you are so *naughty*! I *love* it!" She laughed again and Dehan watched her. Finally she went quiet and sighed. "I love him dearly, Carmen, but he is a pig, an absolute swine, and he does make poor Pam's life a misery. *And* young Charles'. He bullies them mercilessly and takes every opportunity to humiliate them. Frankly . . ." She shook her head, gazing at the heavy black clouds that were building in the north. "I don't know how she's stuck it out all these years."

"Almost forty years."

Bee nodded. "An eternity."

Dehan sat back and raised an eyebrow. "But, Bee, isn't that exactly what you have done?"

"Oh, it's quite different. I am hopelessly in love with him, you see. I have always known what he was like. Ever since he was engaged to my sister . . ."

She left the words hanging, held Dehan's eye. Realization dawned. "You were with him before . . ."

"As soon as I turned sixteen. He knew how I felt. I couldn't resist him. I would have done absolutely anything for him. I still would, even today." She heaved another big sigh. "I am a one-man woman, Carmen, much like you, I suspect. But where you hit the jackpot, I got the booby prize."

"So he was with you when he married Pam . . ."

"I came shortly after."

"Why did he marry her? If he wasn't in love with her . . ." She shrugged and shook her head.

"I've often wondered. He wanted somehow to cock a snook at his father, I suppose."

Dehan shook her head. "No. That doesn't make sense. His father was already dead when he married her."

Bee stared at Dehan a moment and then tapped her head. "Not up here, he wasn't. Charles Sr. and Pam have more in common than you might imagine. Neither of them is capable of letting go. Charles was a rebel, an anarchist, and he wanted more than anything else in the world to be rid and free of his father. He detested his father with a passion. And yet, he never walked away, never sold the castle or the island. Instead he stayed here. Why?"

Dehan spread her hands and shrugged. Bee smiled and went on.

"Here you have a handsome, intelligent, talented, Harvard-educated lawyer. And what does he do when he graduates? He comes to Gordon's Swona and marries the publican's daughter.

"Now, you have the publican's daughter: she is lively, bright, capable, she hates Gordon's Swona, and her great dream is to get away. She marries a man who is a multimillionaire several times over and within a year he has already given her *ample* cause for divorce. She could leave him and walk away with her independence and a small fortune. Does she?" She shook her head. "No, she stays with him for nearly forty years, on Gordon's Swona. I am no psychologist, Carmen, but I think they both have a character flaw. They are weak, what they might call today addictive personalities. But more than that . . ." She gazed away again, toward the French windows. A cloud passed in front of the sun and for a moment it grew dark. "I don't think Charles *knows who he is* without his hatred for his father." She looked back at Dehan. "Once he was free of him, he didn't know what to do. It was as though his fight against his father had *defined* him somehow, and without it he didn't know what to do, or who to be. So he continued that fight, even after he had won, and he married Pam simply to dishonor his father's memory. He certainly didn't love her."

Dehan frowned. "And you think she got some kind of Stockholm syndrome."

"Something like that. Young Charles was born nine months after they were married. He was a lovely, bright, happy baby. She stayed at first because she hoped that the baby would bring them together. It had the opposite effect. He ignored them both and started having affairs, and flaunting those affairs in front of Pam. She became depressed, obviously, threatened to leave him, but somehow lacked the strength. He had alienated all her family and she had nobody to turn to. One month became six, became a year, became ten . . . Now she can't imagine herself without him."

"And you?"

Bee laughed. "Oh, I certainly can't imagine myself without the old goat. I don't even want to. His affairs don't bother me. He was never a very good lover anyway, far too self-absorbed. I just need to be near him, bask in his badness. He is such a naughty man."

Dehan was quiet for a long while, watching Bee. Bee avoided her eye, squinting out at the trees in the hedgerow that were now beginning to toss and bow. Overhead the swallows swooped and skimmed, snatching their tiny prey from the air. Finally Bee said, "I know what you are thinking, Carmen."

"What am I thinking?"

"You're wondering if I slept with the old man."

"And did you?"

She didn't answer for a long moment, then she said, "Well, of course I did. Old Man Gordon was a monster, but he was twice the man his son is." She gave Dehan a mischievous smile. "And a *much* better lover."

Dehan smiled. "And *I'm* naughty . . ."

"Darling, you should have known him. He was so *intense!*"

"So who else did he sleep with?"

"Believe me." She laughed. "There was no sleeping involved." She took a deep breath and shook her head. "I think he made a point of shagging every girl his son was with . . ."

"Even his fiancée."

"*Especially* his fiancée. *Both* of them."

Dehan sighed. "What a family."

"Dysfunctional, toxic . . . all those words pseudo psychologists and social workers love to trot out these days. He was a very bad man, driven by intense passions, appetites, and desires. But he was alive, and when you were with him, dear me! He made *you* feel alive!"

Dehan chewed her lip for a moment, looking up at the sky. "Well, you certainly had all the ingredients necessary for a murder."

Bee studied her for a moment. "Yes, yes, there was that."

"I'm just surprised there hasn't been another one in the last thirty years."

"So far," said Bee, holding her hat with both hands as the wind gusted and the air turned suddenly dark. "We've all wanted him alive, until now." She stood and staggered as another gust caught her. "Darling, the storm is here, let's go inside and have some tea!"

They went inside, closed and secured the French windows, and the mounting gale became a muted bluster. Brown was there setting out the plates, cups, and saucers. He was alone but for the red-haired maid, who was lighting the fire in the huge fireplace. Bee flopped onto the sofa, removed her hat, and started arranging her hair. "Brown, will Mr. Gordon Sr. be joining us?"

"I believe he will, m'lady."

"And where are all the men?" She gave Dehan a smile.

"I'm afraid I don't know, m'lady. A little while ago I served coffee to young Mr. Gordon, the major, and Mr. Stone in here. But I am not sure where they have gone. Shall I go and look for them, m'lady?"

"No, thank you, Brown, no doubt they'll show up before long."

"Very good, m'lady."

He made to leave with the maid in tow when the door opened

and the massive form of Charles Gordon Sr. filled the doorway. He ignored Brown and the maid, eyed Bee, and then stared for a moment at Dehan with a look that was nothing short of a leer.

"Good afternoon," he said and moved into the room. Brown and the maid left and closed the door behind them. "Your husband has left you alone and unguarded."

"I don't need guarding, Mr. Gordon."

"Call me Charles, then I can call you Carmen."

Bee sighed and gazed at the flames that were beginning to enfold the logs in the fireplace.

Dehan smiled at Gordon. "That's okay, Mr. Gordon. I still get a kick out of people calling me Mrs. Stone." She smiled down at Bee. "It reminds me I just hit the jackpot."

Gordon gave a humorless grunt. "Good lord!" He moved across the room toward the salver with the decanters on it. "Oh, for the naivety of youth, though I do declare that even when I was at your tender age I was not naïve about love. Were you, Bee?"

"No, Charles, you know I wasn't. You robbed me of all my innocence when I was just sixteen."

He poured himself a whiskey and turned to her with a wolfish grin. "And didn't we both enjoy that!"

They both laughed, but Dehan thought Gordon laughed with more pleasure, and Bee more trying to please. He turned to Dehan. "Believe me, Carmen, naivety is nothing but an inhibitor to pleasure. One lusts after dreams and illusions that can never be realized. How much more satisfying to lust after what is carnal and real!"

She rested her ass on the arm of a chair and raised an eyebrow at him. "Mr. Gordon, I think you are trying to convince me that you are bad. But I don't believe you are bad . . ."

"Oh really?" He leered at her again. "I wouldn't be too sure . . ."

Dehan shook her head. "No. Bad? Bad was Mick Harragan, who raped and murdered my mother while I was forced to watch.

Bad was Maria Garcia, in the first case I ever worked with Stone[1]. She drugged Nelson Hernandez and his three cousins so they were conscious but they couldn't move. She then shot each one of them with a pump-action shotgun before cutting off Nelson's head and balls and placing them in the middle of the table where they were playing poker." She chuckled and shook her head. "No, you're not bad, Mr. Gordon. You're not even naughty. You're a pussycat." She grinned. "But, I'm sorry, my attention drifted, right about the time where the Ivy League heir to daddy's fortune was going to explain to the Bronx-born and -bred Jewish-Latina detective all about naivety, reality, and carnality. Please, go ahead and educate me, Mr. Gordon."

Bee squealed with laughter and reached out and grabbed Dehan's hand. "Oh, Charles, I do believe you have been put firmly in your place."

Gordon stared at Dehan with baleful eyes. "I am not amused, Mrs. Stone."

Dehan stood. "Get back in the sandpit, Charlie. I eat men for breakfast who make you look like a sissy's bitch. I'm going to find my husband. You may have seen him around. He's a man." She grinned and held out her hands like she was holding two watermelons. "And he has balls."

With that she stepped out of the drawing room, left Bee wiping the tears of laughter from her eyes, and took her attitude across the hall to the study, where she had an accurate hunch she would find me.

What can I say, I guess I'd hit the jackpot too.

---

1. See *An Ace and a Pair*.

NINE

CHARLES, THE MAJOR, AND I HAD LEFT OUR COFFEE TO get cold in the drawing room and crossed the hall to the study. The door, like the drawing room door, was solid walnut with a brass lever handle and a Chubb lock underneath. Charles pushed it open and stood back for me and the major to go in.

"This is where it happened," he said.

I stepped inside and stopped to have a look around. The room was large and roughly square, though perhaps a little wider than it was deep. I estimated it was almost thirty feet across, and twenty-something from the bay window on the right, at the front of the house, to the wall at the back, on my left. The window, flanked on the right by a credenza, overlooked the drive, and opposite, in the center of the wall, there was a large granite fireplace, about six feet high and five feet across, with a large iron grate backed with red firebricks, blackened by centuries of burning wood. It was laid with large pine logs on a bed of kindling. On either side of it there was an old, burgundy Chesterfield. The floor was carpeted in deep, red Wilton.

The far wall, opposite the door, was taken up with a dark mahogany bookcase. In front of that, almost dead center of the room, was a huge oak desk with a black leather chair behind it.

Charles came in and closed the door behind him. I asked, "Is this how it was when he died?"

"Precisely. My father didn't change a thing. And when I took over and started using the study as my own, I didn't see any need to change it. I think this is the best use of the space."

I turned and looked at the door. "A Chubb lock. They are easy to pick."

"Oh, yes, without a doubt."

The major coughed and took a step forward. "Thing is, Detective, if I may, and do remember I was there at the time, the key was still in the lock, which makes it impossible to pick unless you remove the key first. Also, and this was what convinced the police, the latch was in the locked position, and had torn out the wood from the doorframe. Two-hundred-year-old doorframe, I may say. Damn shame." He pointed at a slight discoloration in the wood around the latch. "You can still just see where it was repaired."

I nodded. If Henry had been satisfied that the door was locked, I was satisfied too. I turned back to the desk, then glanced at the two Chesterfields by the fire. The desk was not quite dead center, and the fireplace and the chairs were at a slight, diagonal angle. I looked at the major and pointed at the black leather chair behind the desk. "That's where he was sitting?"

He nodded vigorously. "Exactly. Shall I demonstrate?"

He didn't wait for an answer; in two long, thin strides he was behind the desk, arranging the chair and placing himself in it.

"He was seated, like so, up against the desk as though he had been writing or reading. And in fact, he had on the desk in front of him an open tome on the history of the Scottish clans. He was slumped forward slightly, like so . . ." He leaned forward and allowed his jaw to sag onto his chest. "His left hand was upon the book and his right hand was hanging down by his side. And the revolver was just there . . ." He pointed a couple of feet from the chair. "Lying on the carpet. I shall never forget it. Such an eerie sensation. The oddest things seem to become so important, tiny details stand out, don't they?"

I was staring at the two Chesterfields and asked, absently, "Like what?"

He didn't get up. He stayed in the chair, staring at the ceiling. "Oh, I don't know, foolish things. I remember worrying that Charles would tread dirt and grass into the Wilton, which had just been laid new. Not this one, obviously, a previous one . . . And how red the blood looked on the old man's shirt cuff."

I turned to look at him. "It's true, in those moments our senses are heightened. Which cuff?"

"Eh?"

"Which cuff did you notice the blood on?"

"Oh, yes, his right arm, hanging down. He had two or three large, round drops on his cuff."

"Round?"

"Yes." He nodded. "Quite big and round."

I smiled, moved to the desk, and picked up the stapler. I handed it to him and said, "Pretend this is a gun and hold it to your head as though you are about to shoot yourself in the head."

He looked a bit surprised, glanced at Charles, shrugged, and held the stapler to his head. "Like this?"

"Yup." The door opened. Dehan stepped in and closed it softly behind her. I smiled at her and carried on. "Charles, come here, a bit closer. Now I want you to run a movie in your head, slow motion, okay? Imagine he pulls the trigger. The revolver bucks, a cloud of GSR is instantly ejected by the weapon and covers his hand, his sleeve, his head, and his shoulder. A nanosecond later, the slug impacts his temple, on the horizontal plane, kicks his head to the left, and draws all the blood and gore into the wound with it, while the burning gases from the muzzle sear the edges of the hole and the skin around it. The slug then erupts from the left side of his head, creating a large exit wound and spraying blood and gore out over his left shoulder, the carpet, et cetera. The next instant, his head kicks back to the right, propelled by the force of the exit wound, and simultaneously his hand drops to his side, releasing the gun, and *then*, after the heart has stopped beating, a small amount of blood will ooze from the wound, down the side of his face."

Charles was looking at me with some distaste. "I see."

"Now here's the problem. With his right hand held up and to the *right* side of his head, how did he get large blood droplets on his right cuff?"

Charles' eyebrows shot up and he looked down at the major, who still had the stapler held to his head. I carried on.

"Here's another small problem. Let's say that by some freak of physics, some drops of blood were kicked back onto the cuff. Within half a second, his arm had dropped down by his side; these large droplets are fresh, liquid. By the time, Major, you got to see them, they would not have been circular, they would have been tear-shaped, because the arm was hanging down. So how did they come to be circular?"

"My word . . . !"

I took the stapler from him and set it back on the desk. "But what we have is not a bullet wound on the horizontal plane. We have the bullet entering at an almost forty-five-degree angle. So, Major, can I position you like this, reading a book . . ."

Dehan stepped over to the bookcase, pulled out a large tome, opened it, and set it before the major. I took his hands and placed them with his left forearm resting on the desk and his right wrist as though he were ready to turn the page in a moment or two. Then I took the stapler and went and sat in the Chesterfield on the left of the fireplace and pointed it at his head, as though it were a gun.

"If I were to shoot you from here, we would have just about the correct angle for the entry wound, you would have no GSR on your hand and cuff, the entry wound would not be scorched, and, as you sagged forward, a few droplets of blood might well fall on your cuff. What do you say, Dehan?"

She was nodding as I spoke. "I'd say, given the characteristics of the wound, and the absence of GSR, that is pretty much how it went down. But if that's correct, you have one hell of a problem. Unless he was shot by someone from the Enterprise who was then beamed up, I don't know what happened to your shooter."

I nodded back. "That is, indeed, the problem." I looked at Charles. "But I have to say, Charles, in my opinion there can be no doubt that your grandfather was shot while he was reading, from over here."

The major was frowning. "Well that makes perfect sense, but, as um . . . um . . ." He squinted at Dehan. "Dianne says, what happened to the blighter who shot him?"

I stood and looked around the room slowly while Dehan spoke. "Right down to basics, Stone, if you kill somebody in a locked room, you have to stay in the locked room with them. That is the whole basis of the locked room problem, right?"

"Right."

"So, either one, there is a concealed exit, two, he was killed from outside, or three, the room was locked from outside after the killing. There is no fourth alternative."

Charles gestured toward the chair where I had been sitting. "Well, we have already seen that the shot came from over there. The only way the shot could have come from outside would have been through the window, in which case the window would have been either open or broken, and the shot would have entered the *other* side of his head, which it didn't. So that leaves either a secret exit, or the door being locked from the outside, after the murder."

The major nodded doubtfully. "Houses of this period did have secret passages, often . . ."

I pointed at the bay window. "That goes straight out onto the drive." I pointed to the door. "That leads into the hall, so that would make no sense. That wall there"—I pointed at the huge bookcase—"leads out to the steps down to the kitchen, which leaves only that wall there, where the fireplace is . . ."

I looked at Charles. He shook his head. "That leads onto the ballroom and a brook cupboard, I'm afraid. The police did a very thorough search for secret doors and passages. Your friend, Green, he was convinced, like you, that it was murder. But they never found anything. I'm afraid the secret passage theory is a nonstarter. There is simply nowhere to put one."

Dehan sighed. "Which leaves the theory that the room was locked from the outside *after* the murder."

I returned to the Chesterfield, sat, and gazed at the major a moment. "What time did Charles Sr. go in to see his father?"

"Midmorning, around eleven o'clock."

"They talked for over an hour. Then . . ." I looked at Charles. "Your father came out, went running to the kitchen, hugged Cook, and spread the good news, before leaving to tell Pam about his father's change of heart. He was gone two hours, which brings us to about two o'clock, when he returns, and as he approaches, through the window he sees Old Man Gordon sitting at his desk . . ."

Dehan said, "Which gives us a window from twelve o'clock, when Charles Sr. last saw his father, to two o'clock, when he returned and saw him through the window."

I looked at her, thought a moment, and then carried on. "He entered the hall and presumably came straight to his father's study. Did anybody see him?"

The major shook his head. "Not at that stage. I was out on the lawn chatting with Bee. We saw Charles Sr. arrive down the drive and go into the house, and as far as I know the staff were all in the kitchen. First anyone knew about Charles trying to get into the study was when the butler heard him kicking down the door."

I nodded. "So Charles kicked open the door, rushed in, and found his father as you have described him, with his arm hanging down and the revolver on the floor."

"That's correct."

"Was it normal for Charles Sr. to lock the door?"

The major nodded. "Oh yes, he used to have . . . um . . ."

He glanced at Charles Jr., who smiled. "It's all right, Major.

My grandfather used to have affairs, and he would often have private conversations with them on the telephone, so it was quite normal for him to have the door locked. Also, when he worked, he didn't like to be disturbed. However, apparently my father knocked several times and got no reply, and that was when he became alarmed."

Dehan said, "So he rushed in, found his father, and how long transpired then before you and the staff arrived, Major?"

"Oh, not more than a minute, probably less. When I got here, the butler had already arrived and Charles was just standing there, by the desk, staring down at his father. Terrible thing for a young lad to see. Shocking."

"And the lock was busted."

He glanced over at the door, as though to confirm it had been busted, and nodded. "Yes."

Dehan scratched her head. "So in that scenario, while your father was away talking to Pam, somebody came into the study, took your father's gun, shot him, arranged it to look like suicide, slipped out, and used some thin pliers or a similar tool to turn the key from the outside."

Charles raised his eyebrows and nodded. "If you're right, and it was murder, that would seem to be the only way it could be done. I can't see any other." He frowned, shook his head, and gave an incredulous laugh. "But who on Earth . . . ? It would have to be one of the staff, the major here, or Bee!"

The major goggled in alarm at Charles. I smiled and shook my head. "Not necessarily. There are actually a number of potential candidates for prime suspect. But we can discuss that later if you're inclined. It's actually another question that's playing on my mind."

Charles looked worried. "What's that?"

"Did your grandfather keep his revolver in his study?"

He made a face and shook his head, then turned to the major. The major had gone very serious and was staring at the window. "Reggie?"

He shook his head. "No. Kept it in his room."

I nodded, then looked at Dehan. "It's not like the States here, Dehan. People don't keep weapons for self-defense or home protection. Especially in a place like this, am I right?"

Charles nodded. "Absolutely. Unheard of."

I went on. "If you held on to a weapon like that, you'd have it as a souvenir, and you'd keep it unloaded. You wouldn't have it lying around in a drawer in your study."

"But the old man wasn't British. He was from Boston."

I nodded and smiled. "Not Texas. In any case, the weapon was in his bedroom. So whoever brought it down and shot him with it knew where to look for it."

Suddenly the major stood. He was scowling and his face had gone scarlet. "Look here!" he said. "This has got a bit out of hand, hasn't it? Next thing we'll be accusing . . ." He stammered a moment, then changed tack. "The case was closed and the coroner found it was suicide. They must have known what they were talking about!" Now he met my eye. "No disrespect or anything, but we don't need you Americans coming over and telling us how to investigate a . . . a . . . *suicide*!"

And with that, he marched across the room, wrenched open the door, and stormed out.

Charles' cheeks were flushed. "I am so sorry. You must think us awfully rude. I can't apologize enough . . ."

I shook my head. "No need, I assure you."

"I can't think what came over him. He's normally such a . . ."

I interrupted him. "I met Robert Armstrong. He drove us back from the pub, as far as the gate."

He looked confused. "As far as the gate . . . ?"

"He said he wouldn't set foot in here, and he might have a surprise for you. How serious do you think he might be?"

He laughed. "Old Bobby? That's ridiculous! He's been our gardener for donkey's years!"

"How long, exactly?"

"Oh, exactly? Um, over thirty years. Since before my grandfather died. My grandfather adored him, cared for him and his mother like family. Well, he thought they *were* family. Got a temper, mind, like most Scotsmen, but I wouldn't pay too much attention to him. Probably just in a huff." He hesitated. "Well, I have a few things to attend to before dinner, so . . . Thank you so much, it has been most, um . . . instructive . . ."

TEN

WE LEFT HIM IN HIS STUDY AND STOOD A MOMENT IN the darkened hallway. Outside, the sky had grown dark and a wild wind was making the house groan and the doors and windows creak and bang. Brown, the butler, emerged from the drawing room and made his way silently toward the kitchen with a tray of dirty cups and plates. We had missed tea. I looked at Dehan. She was staring across the hall at the glass panes in the door. Through them you could see the tall pines bowing and tossing under the gunmetal clouds.

I turned away and looked behind me. Under the arch where the staircase divided to climb toward the east wing of the house were the broad double doors that led into the ballroom, and just before them there was a smaller, single door in the wall. I moved over to it and opened it. It was six or seven feet across and a good twelve feet deep. It held buckets and mops, brooms, a couple of vacuum cleaners, and a floor polisher, and along the back wall and all along the right-hand wall there were shelves holding refuse sacks, cloth dusters, cans of polish, feather dusters, and myriad other things you need to keep an old castle looking neat. Behind me I heard Brown's voice.

"Can I help you, sir?"

I nodded, then turned to look at him. "These shelves, the ones along the side here, how long have they been up?"

He looked startled. "For as long as I can remember, sir!"

I smiled. "And how long would that be?"

His eyes seemed to glaze. "I am sixty-two, sir, and my mother worked at the castle before the first Mr. Gordon bought it. The shelves were there when I was a small boy, so well over fifty years."

"Do you mind if I have a closer look at them?"

He frowned but said, "Not in the least, sir. The light switch is there, on the left. Can I help in any way?"

"I don't think so." I snapped on the light and made a careful examination of the fell length of the bottom shelf, and then the middle shelf. When I'd finished, I emerged, closed the cupboard, and gave him another smile. "You've already been very helpful. Thank you. I think we'd like to see the ballroom, if that's okay."

"By all means, sir. It's through there."

He indicated the door. I opened it and followed Dehan in, closing the door behind me. It wasn't palatial, but it was big and largely empty. The floor, like the entrance hall, was black-and-white checkerboard. It was roughly thirty feet across and a good forty or forty-five deep. The ceiling was high and domed, with a spectacular crystal chandelier suspended from the center. A small dais against the right wall allowed for an orchestra or a band, and the far wall was taken up by two sets of broad French windows that gave access to a rear stone terrace with steps down to the gardens. Gardens which a couple of hours earlier had been bathed in warm sunshine, but were now engulfed in shadow while a dark, North Atlantic gale moaned among the chimney stacks and gables. Dehan sighed loudly.

"You have all this, and you still find reasons to kill people."

I smiled and turned my back to the French windows. As I spoke my voice came back at me with a hollow echo. "Enough of this weather might drive me to murder." I started pacing slowly across the room, studying the wall. "Siddhartha, Gautama

Buddha, said that everything in this world is always unsatis-factory."

Dehan crossed the floor to look out the windows. Her voice reverberated down at me out of the dome. "I bet he was invited to all the parties. Didn't they cast him as Eeyore in Winnie the Pooh?"

I kept smiling to myself and nodded. "Yup!"

We both turned. She looked at me with one eyebrow raised. The silver, pre-storm light lay silvery blue across the planes of her face, making her look oddly like a Norse daemon. "They did?"

"No." There was a small couch beside a potted palm up against the wall. I sat on it and considered her where she stood, half in shadow, half ghostly silver-blue. "He said that we are driven by craving and aversion. We perpetually either need some-thing we haven't got: a wife, a husband, a castle, a fortune, freedom . . . Or we want to be free of something we have but don't want: a wife, a husband, a father, a mother, a prison, poverty . . . You know. All those things people kill for. He called it 'dukkha' and said it was the source of all pain and suffering in the world. It was one of his four basic truths."

She made a face, then shoved her hands in her pockets, turned her back to the windows, and fell into darkness.

"So if you want to be happy, all you have to do is stop wanting good stuff and stop caring about the bad shit that happens in life. Good luck with that."

"There is something wrong here, Dehan."

Her disembodied voice said, "What do you mean?"

I chewed my lip and shook my head. "I don't know."

"Cool."

"Walk through it with me."

"Weren't you the one saying we were on honeymoon?"

"Mm-hm . . ." I nodded absently, not really listening. "Who gained from his death?"

She paced away from the window, deeper into shadow, looking down at her feet. "The obvious prime suspect is Charles

Gordon Sr. He had the most to gain. Freedom to marry the girl he loved and inheritance of a major fortune."

"But?"

She stopped, still staring at her feet, and nodded slowly, then shrugged. "But he didn't really love her, though he married her anyway, and by all accounts he had resolved his conflict with his father. He was still the heir."

"Who else?"

She turned and paced back toward the silver-blue glow from the French windows. She said simply, "Pam."

I nodded. "She stood to gain a lot from marrying Charles Sr."

She glanced at me, then back at her feet. "But I think it's a bit more complex than that."

I smiled. "You picked up on that, huh?"

"She was playing them both. While Charles Sr. was away at college in Boston, she was playing Laird and Lady with the old man. I figure she was thinking that if the son was only along for the ride, if you'll excuse the pun, daddy, with his love of all things Scottish, might just jump at the chance of a young, beautiful wife. But then Charles graduates, comes back to the castle, and his daddy tells him she is the wrong class and not from one of the great clans. Bombshell. So she decides to eliminate the old man."

"Hmm . . ."

"And there's another thing." She pointed at me. "If she was a frequent visitor to the master bedroom, she might well have known where he kept the revolver."

"It's a nice theory, but there is one flaw in it."

"What?"

"Charles had just told her that the old man had given him the green light to marry her."

She nodded. "That is not such a big flaw, Stone. In the first place, by now she knows what a temperamental son of a bitch the old man can be. There is no telling when he'll change his mind again. Add to that the fact that she must have known, as everybody did, about the old man's love affair with the Armstrong family, and you have two powerful motives for murder: one, that he might at any time disinherit Charles and her with him, and two, jealous anger. Two gets you twenty that the old man was involved with Mama Armstrong, and as you have said more than once, hell hath no fury like a woman scorned."

"That is a very compelling theory, Dehan. Who else?"

"Bee has to be up there."

"You think so?"

She frowned at me and nodded, then began pacing into the shadows again, toward the dais.

"I had a chat with Bee before I joined you in the study. She's been in love with Charles Sr. since she was a kid. But, get this, she also had an affair with his dad. In fact, according to her, his dad warmed the sheets with just about every woman Charles Sr. was involved with."

I sighed. "I can't say I'm all that surprised. If Oedipus had lived in this house, he would have needed a shrink. But explain to me how that would give Bee motive to kill him?"

She sat next to me on the small divan and put her elbows on her knees. "Revenge. For giving the man she loved permission to marry . . ." She shrugged with one shoulder. "Not just marry, but marry a publican's daughter. It was the ultimate rejection and humiliation, the ultimate insult to her and her sister. Her sister was the right woman for Charles. With her dead, Bee should have stepped into her shoes. But instead . . ."

I nodded. "But instead he allows him to marry this slapper."

She frowned. "Slapper?"

"A London term for a loose woman. You have a point. And revenge gives us one more suspect, perhaps two."

"Mother Armstrong and her son. But that is a lot of speculation, Stone. We don't know how close they really were."

I made a face that was skeptical. "How old would you say Armstrong was? Fifty-six? Fifty-eight? That makes him about sixteen or seventeen at the time of Old Man Gordon's murder. If he heard about the old man's change of heart, which he might well have done if he was working here as the gardener, that gives him a powerful motive . . ."

She nodded. "True." She nodded again, raising her eyebrows. "Especially if he thought the old man had already changed the will."

I pointed at her. "That will. That will is at the heart of all this, Dehan, and I'll tell you something else. It is still a powder keg. I have a bad feeling. I don't think we've heard the last of this."

She frowned. "What do you mean?"

"I can't put my finger on it, but I have a prickling at the back of my neck that says . . ." I hesitated.

Her frown deepened. "What?"

"Dehan, I have a bad feeling. I think there is going to be another murder."

"What? C'mon! You're suffering from a combination of work deprivation and Scottish brooding."

I laughed. "Maybe you're right."

"I'll tell you what we're going to do. We're going to change for dinner, I'm going to slip into my ravishing red with the split up to my hip, we are going to have martinis before dinner, and we are going to forget all about Old Man Gordon and these crazy people. And tomorrow . . ." She leaned across and stabbed my chest with her finger. "As soon as this storm has blown itself out, we are going to take that ferry and spend a day visiting distilleries and remote towns and thinking about something that is *not* a cold case." She spread her hands. "Honeymoon, right? And these guys have Scotland Yard. It was called that for a reason, you know!"

I laughed out loud.

She laughed too. "To deal with crazy Scots murderers!"

"You're right. Hey, you want to dance?"

"Now? Without music?"

"I have a respectable baritone and I can hum a Strauss waltz with the best of them. But you have to put your feet on mine so I can guide you and not tread on your toes."

We did a couple of circuits of the ballroom, with Dehan

standing on my feet and laughing helplessly while I twirled and pranced and hummed the "Blue Danube," and the gale did its best to drown out my respectable baritone. After the second circuit, the door opened and a large figure stood silhouetted, watching us. I came to a halt, and Dehan stepped off my shoes and turned to look, still giggling quietly.

I couldn't make out his features, but I could see it was Charles Gordon Sr. After a moment he spoke.

"My son tells me you've been inquiring about my father's death."

"As a matter of fact, we were. We run the cold-cases unit at our precinct and we were curious. We didn't mean to intrude."

He remained immobile. It was unsettling not to be able to see his face or his expression. After a moment, he said, "It's not a cold case. It was ruled suicide."

"So I understand. As I say, it was just a passing interest."

He took a step into the room. "You think it was not suicide?"

The hairs on the back of my neck bristled. I took a step toward him, partially blocking Dehan. I kept my voice level. "There are details that are hard to explain: the absence of powder burns, the absence of gunshot residue, the angle of the shot . . ."

"You don't need to convince me, Stone." He took another step closer and now the gray light from the French windows touched half his face. One eye peered at me, hard, calculating. "I said it was murder from the start. The inspector agreed with me. But he was overruled. They closed it as a suicide." He shook his head. "My father would not have committed suicide, not in a million years."

I nodded, then shrugged. "Well, as I say, Mr. Gordon, we just had a passing interest because of our work back home . . ."

Dehan stepped forward. "Did you ever suspect anybody?"

"Mrs. Stone . . ." For a moment it sounded like an answer to his question and I frowned, confused. Then he said, "Yes, I had my ideas, but I was never able to confirm them. You know what they say . . ." He shifted slightly in the shadows, and I knew he was looking at me again. "Keep your lovers close, but keep your enemies closer."

He turned and moved back to the open door. There he paused and spoke, out into the hallway. "We'll be dressing for dinner." Then a poisonous smile leached into his voice. "The Camerons will be joining us again. Such a charming couple."

He disappeared toward the stairs, and we heard his heavy tread climbing toward the upper floor.

I scratched my head. "You think we could cross to the mainland this evening? I'll take my chances with the storm."

She leaned her forehead on my chest, laughing softly. "Stone! Where have I brought us? What are they like?"

"Come on, let's go get changed. I need a drink. And tomorrow we go spend a day back in the real world. Maybe when we get back, this lot will seem a bit more normal."

She looked up at me and nodded. "I guess it was our fault for asking questions in the first place."

"I guess."

I gave her a kiss and we made our way into the hall. The storm had graduated from moaning and groaning to the occasional scream and wail. We had just reached the landing, where the stairs divided and climbed to the east and west wings, when behind us the door burst open and the howl of the wind filled the hall, and throughout the house we heard doors bang and slam. We turned to look. I was surprised to see it was Robert Armstrong. He wrestled the door closed, then stood watching us a moment. Finally he said, "Ah've buznezz wuth Gordon."

I asked, "Father or son?"

He shook his head. "Na'ye mind. Ah ken the way."

He stood watching us, waiting. We turned and continued up to our room.

ELEVEN

SOMEBODY HAD LIT THE FIRE IN OUR ROOM. AS WE LET ourselves in, the first flash of lightning lit up the gardens outside and showed a low, oppressive ceiling of dense, dark gray cloud. Less than a second later, the heavens split and exploded, the lights went out, and a second flash illuminated the world with strange jerky, violet light. The flames in the fire wavered and the lights flickered and came back on.

Dehan muttered something foul in Spanish, closed the door, and made her way to the bathroom, stripping off her blouse.

We showered and dressed with the storm tearing up the sky outside and claps of thunder threatening to smash down the roof, but there was no rain, only the prickling static of the humid, sultry air, and the trees bending and swaying through the window in the wild wind, caught occasionally in that eerie, stuttering light.

I went from the bathroom back into the bedroom, pulled on my dress pants and my wing-collared shirt, and poured myself a whiskey. While I was trying to tie my bow tie in the mirror above the fire, I heard Dehan behind me. "If I'm Miss Scarlet, does that make you Colonel Mustard or Reverend Green?"

I turned and told myself silently I must be the luckiest man on Earth. She did a slow turn for me. It was scarlet silk, low cut at the front and insanely low cut at the back. And then there was the slit, all the way up to her hip. She had her hair in a bun and a single pearl at her throat. I raised an eyebrow at her.

"What kind of demon are you?" I said. "I forbid you to wear that outside this bedroom. In fact," I added, stepping closer, "I forbid you to wear it *in* this bedroom. Take it off. Immediately . . ."

She took hold of my bow tie and started to tie it. "Behave," she said.

"I intend to, very badly . . ."

The sky ripped open again, diabolical dancing trees springing at us through the leaded panes against the electric blue and inky turmoil of the sky. And then there was the first patter of rain on the glass.

Dehan glanced at the window, then frowned at me. "Listen. Is it the wind . . . ?"

Through the rattles, the moans, and the groans, I heard another sound. At first it was like a bark, but then Dehan said, "Shouting," and walked quickly to the door. She opened it and stepped out. I followed her down the dark corridor to the galleried landing. There, in the hall, was Cameron. He was standing, legs akimbo, pointing savagely in the direction of the study. The study and whoever was in the doorway were both out of sight, but the light from the open door was playing on Cameron's face, and the expression was unmistakable rage. His voice was raised, but he was controlling it, and there didn't seem to be anybody with him.

"I've had enough!" he said. "I've had enough of being humiliated by your damned family! I'll no' take it anymore, d'you understand? I'll no' *take* it anymore! Yiz can all go to hell! And take the bitch wuth you!" He took a step forward and his face twisted into a snarl. "But don't think you'll get away wuth ut! Believe me, you'll no get away wuth thus! I'll make you pay, so help me God! I will *make you pay!*"

He turned and stormed across the hall, wrenched the door open, and turned again, pointing savagely at whoever stood, silent and out of sight. "I will *destroy* you! So help me God, *I will fucking destroy you!*"

And with that, he stepped out into the storm and slammed the door behind him.

We returned to our room and, in silence, Dehan finished tying my bow and I pulled on my jacket. Then we went down the stairs in the uncertain, flickering light of the lamps. The study was closed when we got to the bottom, but from the drawing room we could hear voices. I opened the door and followed Dehan in.

It was like a slightly edited version of the night before. Bee was seated on the sofa in turquoise Chinese silk, holding a gin and tonic, gazing at the fire with miniature flames dancing inside her glass. She glanced at us and gave a smile that was on the weary side of tired.

Pam was seated in a chair facing us, wearing unremarkable black velvet and holding a glass of beer. When she saw Dehan, she avoided her eye and looked away at the burning logs. I was surprised to see Sally Cameron there after the scene we'd just witnessed in the hall. She was standing, with her wild red hair gathered in a bow, where she had been the night before, at the French windows, but now she was looking out at the storm through the rain-spattered panes.

And tonight it was the major who was at the drinks salver, looking over his shoulder at us, holding a decanter and a balloon glass.

But the main difference was that Charles Gordon Jr. was not there. His father was standing where Ian had been the night before, beside Sally. I watched his eyes travel over Dehan, then shift to me. They were not hard to read. They were hostile and hard.

The major was the first to speak, with no trace left of his earlier outburst. "Ah! The honeymoon couple! What can I get you to drink? Mrs. Stone, what is your fancy?"

He poured a generous measure of cognac and hurried across

the floor to hand it to Gordon Sr. Then he stood grinning expectantly at Dehan.

She winked at him. "You know what, Reggie? Why don't I come over there and show you how *I* mix a martini?"

He stammered something and she took his arm and led him away. I glanced at Gordon, who was still watching me. "Jr. not joining us tonight, Mr. Gordon?"

"I neither know nor care, Mr. Stone. He is a huge disappointment to me, so I try to avoid him."

Bee sighed. "He had some business to attend to with the gardener chap, Armstrong. He said he'd join us a little later."

I frowned at her. "Bobby Armstrong?"

She looked curious. "Yes, why?"

"I saw Armstrong arrive, but that was almost an hour ago. I thought I heard him talking to Ian just ten minutes ago."

She shrugged. "Perhaps he's finished then. No doubt he'll join us presently."

I glanced at Sally. She hadn't turned around. Gordon was still watching me. Now he smiled. It wasn't a pretty sight. "That detective's mind never stops whirring, does it, Mr. Stone?"

"Never."

He leered. "You should be careful. They say that can be a terrible strain on a marriage. It can drive a partner into a lover's arms."

I smiled at him. Dehan approached with two martinis and handed me one. I took it and said, "There are lots of things that can do that, Gordon." I sipped, winked at Dehan. "That's perfect." Then I turned back to Charles Sr., still smiling. "One of them is being an asshole."

Bee spluttered and sprayed gin and tonic over her blue dress, and Pam's shoulders began to shake as she tried to suppress her laughter. Before he could answer, I went on.

"I have been a homicide detective, in the Bronx, for over twenty-five years. You can imagine that during that time I have met and interrogated some very bad people, cruel and psychotic people. I have lost track of how many, but it must run into many hundreds. They all lied to me, and they all insulted me at one time or another. So I have grown over time to be insensitive to insults, however subtle, and damned good at knowing when people are lying to me."

The major stammered for a moment, standing behind Pam's chair, then blurted out, "It must be fascinating work!"

I made a "not so much" face. "It's not like the movies or the TV. Even the ones that aim to be realistic have to elaborate and glamorize things, because the vast majority of homicides are . . ." I thought about it for a moment and shook my head. "Tragically banal. Time of death is almost impossible to tell in the real world, DNA and fingerprints can take up to three months to get back from the lab, and"—I paused for effect—"ninety percent of murders are committed by a member of the family or a close friend. The motive is almost always sexual jealousy, anger, or greed." I gave a small, dry laugh. "Millions of people every year spend thousands of dollars protecting their homes and their children against outsiders who might break in through the window or the back door, when statistically the real threat already lives in the house."

Right on cue, a gust of wind rattled the glass in the windows, a flash of lightning lit up the night, and a clap of thunder smashed open the sky, then rolled away across the black ocean. When it had passed, there was some nervous laughter and Bee said, "My goodness! With timing like that, you should be on the stage."

Sally turned away from the window to stare at me, and Gordon said, "Are you telling me that my father was probably killed by somebody in his own household?"

Dehan went and stood beside the major, behind Pam's chair. She answered for me.

"You'd be in a better position to know that, Mr. Gordon. We've only been here twenty-four hours and his death was almost forty years ago. You and the inspector were convinced it wasn't suicide, so you must have had somebody in mind."

The major swallowed hard, staring at his feet. Bee uncrossed her legs, then sighed and crossed them again, like she was losing patience with their limited range of positions. Pam was staring hard at her husband, and Sally went to the drinks salver and started mixing herself another drink.

Gordon said, "Is it really only twenty-four hours? It seems so much longer."

Sally spoke suddenly in a loud voice: "Jealousy and greed?"

Rain rattled on the windows. She dropped ice in her glass, then spilled in the gin. The tonic fizzed loudly. The whole room waited. She turned to face Gordon. "Who in this household could possibly have felt jealousy, or greed?" Then she turned and raised an eyebrow at me. "I think this murder, if it *was* murder, Mr. Stone, must fall in the ten percent of 'other motives.' But most likely, you know, it was just suicide, like the police said. Is there not something to be said for leaving well enough alone?"

I gave her my sweetest smile. "We're just here on our honeymoon, Mrs. Cameron."

The dining room door opened and Brown stepped in. He surveyed the room and finally his eyes rested on Gordon Sr. "Should I serve dinner now, sir? Mr. Gordon Jr. is still in his study, it seems."

Pam turned in her chair to look at him. "Have you called him?"

Brown came farther into the room so she didn't have to crane to see him. "Yes, madam. There is no answer."

Pam looked at Gordon. Gordon shrugged and sipped his drink. "I'm starving. Serve it now as far as I'm concerned."

There was a howl and a shriek and the wind seemed to grow louder. The drawing room door and the windows rattled. I frowned at Dehan.

She said, "Was that the front door?"

Bee stared at her. "Who on Earth would come in at this time of night, in this weather? Has Charles been out?" The howl subsided. Lightning lit up the gardens outside, momentarily silhouetting the trees. Thunder rolled, then split the sky. When it passed, we heard the savage hammering: once, twice, a third time. The major exclaimed, "What the devil . . . ?"

And then there was a shout, half-hysterical, from the hall.

"*Help! Help! Fer God's sake! Somebody! Help!*"

Pam was on her feet and running, gasping, "*Charles!*" I was ahead of her, wrenching open the door, running across the checkerboard hall toward the study. The door was open, light streaming out. In it I saw, as I ran, where the latch had been smashed, ripped from the wood.

I stopped dead in the portal, blocking the doorway, taking in the scene. Pam was clawing at my back, screaming at me to move, to let her through. I turned and enfolded her in my arms, pushing her back. "Major! *Major!* Take her to the drawing room. Lock her in if you have to. Gordon! Get out of here! Take your wife away from here! *Now!*"

But Gordon just stood staring at me. The major was gaping. Pam was hysterical, thrashing, struggling to get to the room. I looked at Dehan. She slipped past in her scarlet dress and entered the study. I heard her snap, "Back up. Move away from the desk. Don't touch anything."

Across the hall, I saw Bee and Sally come out of the drawing room door and stand staring at us. I grabbed Pam's shoulders in my hands and shook her, staring into her face. She was still screaming, "*What has happened? Let me get in there! It's my son! For God's sake! What's happened? Let go of me!*"

I shook her again. "Pam! Pam, listen to me! You cannot go in there! Charles has been shot. He needs my help. The longer you keep screaming, the longer it is before I can help him. Do you want me to help him, or do you want him to die?"

Gordon Sr. went white and stepped toward me. I looked him in the eye and said, "Don't even think about it, pal."

He stopped dead. Pam was goggling at me. I looked her in the eye again and said, "Do you want your son to die, Pam?"

She shook her head. "Of course not!"

"Then go with the major and your husband and wait in the drawing room while Detective Dehan and I do what we can to help him. Go! Now! Every second is vital!"

I propelled her gently toward the major. He put his arm around her and I pointed at the drawing room door. "Go!"

They withdrew reluctantly across the hall and into the drawing room. I turned and went into the study.

It was an eerie sight, like a strange, physical manifestation of the scene I had visualized just a few hours before. Only there were some significant differences between the scene I had imagined and the scene I was looking at. For a start, it wasn't Old Man Gordon who was sitting behind the desk in the large leather chair with his brains blown out. It was Charles Gordon Jr., his grandson.

The left side of his head wasn't missing, it was just spread out all over the Wilton carpet, part of his desk, and most of his left shoulder—that part was the same—and like his grandfather, he was slumped forward slightly, gaping at a ledger on his desk, with his right arm hanging limp down by his side. On the floor, a couple of feet from his chair, was a revolver. It looked like an old Smith & Wesson .38, Military and Police model.

Dehan was hunkered down looking at it, and behind her, staring wide-eyed and pale, was Bobby Armstrong.

TWELVE

THE DOOR HAD A BIG, MUDDY BOOT PRINT JUST BELOW the handle. I could see the mud was wet. Dehan was on her hands and knees, sniffing the muzzle of the revolver. Then she touched it gently with the backs of her fingers. She stood and said to me, "You got your cell?"

I nodded and pulled it from my pocket. There was no signal. I looked at Armstrong. "You got any signal?"

He shook his head like I was crazy. "Och, there's no signal here in a storm! An' who're you going t'call, anyhoo?"

"There are no cops on the island?"

"Ut's a private island. What for, anyway? Nothin' ever happens here!"

"Just a murder every forty years."

"Ah didna kill him!"

"I didn't say you did."

Dehan said, "What's 911 here?"

"999." I picked up the phone on the desk, listened, and shook my head. "The line is dead."

Armstrong curled his lip. "What did yiz uxpect, in a storm like thus?"

"What are you doing here, Armstrong? You said today you

wouldn't come past the gate. Yet this is the second time I've seen you in the house since then."

He snarled at me. "Ah don't have to answer your feckin' questions! Yer nay a cop here, see?"

I jerked my head toward the door. "Get out. Go wait in the drawing room with the others."

He took a step toward me. "Ah don't have to do what you feckin' tell me, pal!"

"This is a crime scene, *pal*! You're disturbing the evidence. Right now my testimony and Detective Dehan's is likely to clear you of suspicion. Disturb the scene or leave the house, and you go right to the top. Am I getting through to you, Armstrong?"

He muttered something about "Feckin' Yanks!" and marched across the hall to push through the door into the drawing room. I watched it close behind him and turned back to Dehan. I jerked my head at the gun.

She said, "It smells like it was fired recently, but the muzzle is cold, so it wasn't that recent."

I nodded. "That figures."

She frowned. "It does?"

"Mm-hm . . ." I pulled my cell from my pocket again and photographed the door and the muddy prints that led from it across the Wilton carpet to the side of the desk. "Their nice carpet is getting a lot of punishment. I wonder if they deliberately chose red."

She narrowed her eyes at me and pointed her finger at my chest like a gun. "How did you know?"

I made a face like brain-ache and shook my head. "I didn't. I told you. It was a feeling." I shrugged. "They killed the old man, but none of the issues they had were resolved. It felt like they were all bubbling to the surface again."

She spread her hands. "But why now, almost forty years later?"

I thought about it, chewing my lip. "Maybe for that very reason."

"What is that supposed to mean, Stone? You're being cryptic. You know that makes me mad. And besides, this poor sap wasn't even born when his grandfather was killed."

I smiled at her. "Miss Scarlet in the study with the dinosaur. This is not our case, Miss Scarlet. We have done the Scottish police the courtesy of preserving their crime scene, and now we must graciously withdraw."

She grunted and walked past me to the bay window, examining it carefully.

"You know we are both ignoring the elephant in the room. We should call the doctor."

"You mean the one who was here a little earlier threatening to destroy people? The one whose wife is sleeping with the victim's father? That doctor?"

"Yeah, that one."

I stared at the burning logs in the fire, thinking of Bobby standing in the hall, staring up at us on the stairs. He'd said he had business with Gordon. I'd asked him, "Father or son?"

He'd stood, staring at me, and shaken his head: "Na'ye mind. Ah ken the way."

The flames burned a good three feet high, wavering against the blackened bricks. The wood crackled and sparks showered onto the hearth. Ian Cameron, standing on the black-and-white-checkered floor beneath us, the light from the study door lying slantwise, casting his shadow long behind him. "I will *destroy* you!" he had said. "So help me God, *I will fucking destroy you!*"

I had assumed he was talking to Gordon Sr. It was hard to imagine anybody feeling that strongly toward Gordon Jr. I sighed and turned to Dehan. "Come along, Miss Scarlet. Let's stop messing up the crime scene. It's not ours to mess up."

With a face that was on the mad side of reluctant she moved toward the door and stopped. Brown was there, staring at Gordon Jr. with tears in his eyes. He looked up at Dehan. "Mr. Gordon, madam . . ."

Dehan seemed nonplussed for a moment. I stepped toward him and said, "He's been shot, Brown."

He frowned at me, struggling to understand. "Who . . . ?"

"We don't know. We have to wait until the police arrive."

He looked around the room. "It's the same . . ."

I nodded. "Almost exactly the same."

"They'll put it down to suicide again. But Mr. Gordon wouldn't, sir. I know he wouldn't."

Dehan stepped closer to him. "What makes you say that?"

His bottom lip curled and the tears spilled from his eyes. "He was happy-go-lucky . . . He wasn't . . ." He pulled the handkerchief from his breast pocket, mopped his eyes, and blew his nose. "Forgive me, sir, but . . ." He spoke quietly, looking at his handkerchief. "He wasn't like the others, if you know what I mean." He looked me in the eye. "He had no . . ." He hesitated, then his face twisted with anger. "He had no *agenda*! He wasn't trying to get anything from anyone, he was happy to take life as it came, day to day."

I nodded. "I understand." I sighed. "Look, we have a very delicate situation here. My wife and I are very experienced police officers, but we have no jurisdiction. This scene must be preserved until the police arrive. The door needs to be sealed. Can you see to that?"

He studied my face for a long moment, then stared at Dehan. "Are we just going to leave him like that?"

I nodded. "I'm afraid we have to, until they arrive."

He took a deep breath. "I understand. I'll find a chain and a padlock, sir, and leave the keys with you."

"That will do fine. Thank you."

He moved to the cupboard by the ballroom, switched on the light, disappeared inside, and reappeared a moment later with a tool kit, a length of chain, and a strong padlock. While he set about securing the door, Dehan and I crossed the hall and pushed into the drawing room.

What we found there was not an attractive sight. Gordon was

in a large armchair by the wall, apart from the rest. He looked pasty and sick. Sally was sitting on the arm of that chair, stroking his head and muttering things to him. They both looked up as we came in. He looked anxious. She looked like she was trying to read us.

Pam had returned to her chair by the fire. She had curled up on herself and had her face in her hands, rocking back and forth in silence. Bee had also returned to her place on the sofa. She looked startled, as though somebody had just shouted at her and she couldn't get over it. She was silent, but she had a small, floral handkerchief and kept dabbing her eyes with it. The major was sitting beside her, frowning resentfully at the fire. I looked for Bob Armstrong. He was in a chair by the library, scowling at the window.

I closed the door and looked at the parents of the dead man. The mother alone, trying to convince herself she had not just slipped into hell, the father across the room being consoled by one of his mistresses. I glanced at Dehan.

"There's a picture of *dukkha* in action if ever I saw one." I looked over at Pam and raised my voice. "Mrs. Gordon, Mr. Gordon . . ." I waited till they were both looking at me. "I am afraid your son is dead. He was murdered at some point during the afternoon or the evening. We are both very sorry."

Pam screamed. It was a scream of pain, deep and visceral. She fell on her knees, clutching her chest with her hands, staring up at the ceiling, her mouth open wide and her wet face flushed almost purple. Bee gasped, not at the news but at the state of Pamela. She rose and went to her, but Pamela turned on her like a savage animal, spitting, "*Get away from me! Get away from me! You murdering, thieving bitch!*"

Then she was on her feet, rushing across the room, screaming at her husband and at Sally, "*Are you satisfied? Are you fucking satisfied? All you ever wanted was to destroy your family! Well now you've done it, you piece of fucking shit!*"

Sally stood. "Pam, for God's sake! He's just lost his son!"

Pamela's neck swelled, her tendons stretched, and her face turned crimson as she screamed in Sally's face, "*My son! My son! My fucking son! Not his! And not yours, you filthy, thieving whore!*"

She gave a small gasp. Her eyes went very wide, and her legs seemed to turn to Jell-O. Dehan stepped over to her and caught her as she keeled over. Between us, we moved her to a couch by the wall and settled her on it. I studied the major's face a moment, then Bee's, and decided she had more of a grip on things.

"Bee, she's in shock. She'll soon start to get very cold. Can you arrange for Brown or one of the maids to bring her a blanket?"

She frowned. "Yes, absolutely. And some tea, I think. A good cup of tea. Pull ourselves together . . ."

She hurried to the bell by the wall and pressed it. Meanwhile, I went to where Gordon was sitting motionless, staring at nothing. I rested my ass on the back of the sofa and watched him a moment.

"Mr. Gordon, are you able to listen to me and take in what I am saying?"

He blinked a few times, then scowled at me. "Yes. Of course I am."

"Our cell phones have no signal, and the landline is dead. There is no way of contacting the police until the storm subsides."

He nodded. "Yes."

"I've had Brown seal the room. It's a crime scene and nothing must be touched until the police get here."

He stared at me like I'd said something outrageous. Then he frowned across the room at where Armstrong was sitting, then back at me. "That could be days," he said. "It could be two or three days before we get a signal, or the ferry can land."

"Well, is there a radio on the island? Surely you have a police station with a radio."

He shook his head. "This is a private island. There is no police station here. And no radio."

I looked at Bob, then at Sally. "What do you do when there is an emergency? What does your husband do if there is an accident, or somebody gets ill? You must have some way of contacting the mainland when there's a storm."

Bob ignored me, Sally shrugged, and Gordon said, "We cope. The way people have always coped out here."

I sighed. "Mr. Gordon, this is not a game. Your son has been murdered and . . ." I hesitated.

He looked up at me, frowning, narrowing his eyes. "What? What aren't you telling me?"

I sighed again and spread my hands. "It is a restaging of your father's murder."

There was no mistaking the horror on his face. His skin looked like a corpse's skin. His eyes bulged and his pupils went to pinpricks. His voice when he spoke was thick. He said, "No . . ."

"I'm afraid so."

He shook his head. "No, this is, this is madness. It can't be. How . . . ?"

Armstrong's voice bellowed across the room. "*How?*" We all looked. He stood and took two steps toward us. "*How?* I'll tell ye fuckin' how! Because *he* done it! He murdered his own feckin' son! Tha's how!"

Sally got to her feet. "Robert Armstrong! What are you talking about?"

"He's a thieving, murdering bastard! Tha's what I'm talking aboot!"

"For your information, Charles has been with me all afternoon and all evening!"

He sneered. "Well, there's a big feckin' surprise! An' where was his wife? Screwin' your feckin' husband? Yiz make me sick to my stomach, the whole disgusting, thieving, filthy lot of yiz!"

Gordon got to his feet. He was trembling violently. "I did not kill my own son . . ."

Armstrong advanced another step. "Do you expect *anyone* here to believe tha'? Do you? Let me tell you something, there is *nothing*! *Nothing!* That you are no' capable of! You are a sick, sick man, Charles Gordon!"

Gordon turned to me. He was sweating profusely. "Find who did this. Find who murdered my son. I will pay you any amount you want. Just name it. But find the man who killed my son. I am the Laird. I am a local magistrate. This island *belongs* to me. I *give* you the jurisdiction. If there are problems when the police arrive, I will assume full responsibility. As of now, I am employing you as private investigators. Find my son's killer and bring him to justice!"

I looked over at Dehan.

She shrugged. "It's not like we're going to be doing much honeymooning."

I grunted. She had a point, and the fact was I was pretty sure I had it cracked already. I just needed to confirm a couple of points before I reeled the killer in. I turned back to Gordon. "All right, Mr. Gordon. You have a deal. But the minute we get a signal, or the landline is fixed, we contact the cops and they take over."

I took a moment to look at everyone in the room. After a moment, I said, "Is there anybody here who objects? Is there anyone who does *not* want me and Detective Dehan to find Charles Gordon Jr.'s killer?"

It's not the kind of question you want to answer in the affirmative. There was no reply at all, and after a moment I turned to Sally. "Where is your husband right now, Mrs. Cameron?"

Her cheeks colored and her eyes were bright. I saw her breathing quicken and she fought hard not to glance at Gordon. "I assume he's at home."

"You had a fight?"

"Why would you say that?"

I raised my eyebrows and waited.

Dehan stepped up beside me and repeated, "Did you have a fight?"

She shrugged. "It was nothing serious. A disagreement."

Gordon groaned and lowered himself into his chair again,

covering his eyes with his hand. I kept my eyes on Sally. "What about?"

"He didn't want to come here tonight. I did."

"And did he?"

"What?"

Dehan said, "Did he come here?"

She hesitated.

Gordon said, "Yes. He did. He was here earlier."

"You spoke to him?"

He nodded, then amended, "It was more a case of him speaking to me."

I nodded a few times, chewing my lip. Finally, I said, "I need him brought here, now. Major . . ."

He stood.

"Will you go with Brown? Bring him here. Do not under any circumstances tell him what has happened. Tell him that Mrs. Gordon is not well, that she needs immediate help. She is distraught and needs sedating. Tell him it is a matter of the utmost importance, and it is very urgent that he comes to the castle straightaway. Can you do that?"

"Yes, yes, of course!"

"Good, go, quickly." He hurried away, calling for Brown, and I turned to face the room. "Okay, now listen up, let me tell you how this is going to work."

I stood and walked to the fireplace, where I could see all of them staring back at me.

"We're going to need to talk to each one of you in turn, to get statements from you. It's going to be slow and tedious, and laborious, but make no mistake, every single one of you in this room is a suspect. And when your own police arrive here, you'll be even more of a suspect, because they won't have had the advantage I have of having spoken to you all already, and got something of your stories.

"So we are going to take each one of you, by turns, into the dining room, get your statement, ask you some questions, and then you'll be free to do whatever you like, except leave this house." I smiled. "Not that there are many places you could go, if you did. Any questions?"

There was no reply, only the howl and scream of the wind and the stuttering flash of light outside the window. While I'd been talking to Gordon, the red-haired maid had brought some tea and a blanket, and Pam had come around and was now sitting huddled on the sofa staring at her husband with no particular expression on her face. I glanced at Dehan and she nodded.

I said, "Mrs. Gordon, do you feel up to answering a few questions?"

She nodded without looking at me. "Let's get it over and done with."

"I don't know if you heard, Brown and the major have gone to get Dr. Cameron. When he gets here, I suggest he gives you a sedative and you try to sleep."

She didn't react. She spoke almost mechanically. "My son is dead. No amount of sedatives can change that. Let's just find that bastard who did it."

She threw off the blanket, got unsteadily to her feet, and we followed her into the dining room.

THIRTEEN

SHE SAT AT THE FOOT OF THE LONG TABLE AND DEHAN and I sat on either side of her. I studied her a moment. She was staring at the tabletop. I was aware that for her in that moment everything seemed unreal, because reality was too painful to face.

I said, "Mrs. Gordon, I think you were still unconscious when I explained this to your husband. It's something very important that you need to understand." She raised her eyes and frowned at me, like she couldn't get how anything but her son's death would ever be important again. I held her eye and said, "Your son's murder was an almost exact reenactment of his grandfather's murder."

Her frown deepened as she struggled to understand what it meant. "But, that can't be . . ."

Dehan leaned forward. "What is it," she asked, "that makes it impossible?"

Pam looked at her quickly, her eyes flicking over her face, like she was trying to fathom why she was asking the question. "Because the old man committed suicide."

I shook my head. "You must realize by now, Pam, that he did not, that he was murdered."

And Dehan added quietly, "And for forty years nobody has been able to work out how. So that means one thing . . ."

Pam stared at her in horror.

I supplied the words that Dehan had left out. "Whoever killed Old Man Gordon may also have killed your son. So I am going to ask you straight-out, Mrs. Gordon. Do you know who killed the old man?"

Her eyes shifted to my face, then drifted to stare at nothing but the nightmare images inside her own head. After a moment she said quietly, "No . . ." but it didn't sound like an answer to my question.

"What does that mean, Mrs. Gordon?"

"I never believed . . ." She looked at Dehan, as though she thought she might understand what she was saying. "I never believed Charles was capable of killing his own father. I knew he resented him. I knew there was a lot of anger, but I always had it in my mind that all that resentment and anger covered up a need to be loved. He didn't want to *kill* him. He wanted to *hurt* him, to make him pay *attention*! That's why I never believed that the old man was murdered."

She looked from me to Dehan and back again, searching for confirmation that what she was saying made sense. I was still wondering what it was exactly that she was saying. She must have seen that because she went on, looking into my eyes.

"I mean, why would he?" Suddenly her face twisted with anger and bitterness. "All he ever wanted was to *hurt* people. That is the joy of life for him! Causing pain and humiliation. Believe me, he would have got far more out of seeing his father's face at our wedding than out of killing the poor old bastard!"

She raised a trembling hand and pointed toward the drawing room. "And if he looks upset now, it's not for the loss of his son! Oh, God no! It's because he won't have him there to torture, torment, and humiliate anymore!"

Dehan leaned forward. "Mrs. Gordon, Pam, I'm a little confused. I'm not sure what you are telling us here. Because on the one hand it sounds as though you're saying Charles Gordon Sr. would not have killed his own father and his son, because he would prefer to torment them, but on the other it sounds as though you're suggesting he did. Can you clarify this for me?"

She closed her eyes, took a deep breath, and gave a long, shuddering sigh.

"I don't know *what* I'm saying." She opened her eyes again, then looked back at Dehan. "I'm telling you I never *believed* that the old man was murdered. *He* was always going on about how it was murder, and the fellow who came up from London. But I never believed it. It didn't make any sense to me. Who would want him dead? But now, you're saying this to me, and the only person who'd had any *kind* of motive was Charles . . . But I can't believe it. His own father, his own *son*!"

I sighed and flopped back in my chair. "Where were you this afternoon and this evening, Mrs. Gordon?"

She gaped at me. Her jaw dropped and her eyes went wide. "You think *I* killed my own *son*?"

I shook my head. "I think that is very unlikely, but I still want to know where you were, because then maybe you can confirm where other people were. If we can nail down everybody's whereabouts up to cocktails, then it won't be hard to spot the person with no alibi. That's the theory, anyway."

She closed her eyes.

"I left you at the inn. That must have been one or one thirty. I'm not sure. I walked back because I wanted to clear my head. I went up to my room and had a wee lie-down. But then, about three or so, *he* came in and said he needed me to leave the bedroom because he was *entertaining*!"

Her face flushed red. I nodded that I understood. "Did he tell you who he was entertaining?"

"He didn't need to." Her face and her voice were savage. "His latest fancy is Sally Cameron. It's not the first time he's had her here, but he's never been quite so blatant about it before."

Dehan raised an eyebrow. "What would make him become blatant like that, do you think?"

The room went very quiet. It was the same question I was about to ask. Pam stared hard at her hands and her jaw worked, but she didn't say anything for a good while. Eventually she shrugged and shook her head. "Old age? Complacency? The knowledge that he can get away with blue bloody murder and nobody will raise a *fucking finger* to stop him?"

I drummed my fingers softly on the table. "It was hard to miss, Mrs. Gordon, that you and he did not draw together when you discovered your son was dead. It was Sally who was consoling him."

"That would be no great surprise to anybody."

"Is it possible that theirs is more than just a passing affair?"

"I've no doubt she believes it is."

"And if she is right, could that be why he has become more blatant?"

She gazed at me with hostile eyes. "What has this to do with my son's murder?"

I nodded several times. It was a good question, and I wasn't sure what the answer was. "So, he asked you to leave the room. What happened next?"

"I dressed and went downstairs. My son and the major were in the drawing room, but I couldn't face seeing people so I went out onto the terrace. Bee came out after me and sat with me. The woman is insufferable. She is forever trying to be *kind* to me, in spite of my low class! I could . . ." She stopped herself and took a deep breath. "She knew that Sally was there. She had arrived with the groceries for the kitchen. Charles has a taste for working-class wenches. No doubt the whole fucking house was gossiping and giggling about Sally making her 'delivery'!"

Dehan asked, "What happened next?"

"We talked for a while. I asked her how she could still love him after the way he had treated her for all these years. She gave me some crap about how she loved him *because* of the way he was. I told her she must be a fuckin' masochist, and she said maybe she was, but she didn't care. She was happy just to be near him."

She gave an ugly smile and snorted. Dehan narrowed her eyes. "What's funny?"

Pam pointed at the drawing room door. Her accent seemed to be getting stronger the madder she got. "That bastard humiliated and broke me, and because of that I've tolerated all the shit that he's thrown at me for nearly forty years. I watched him break my son's spirit, I watched him parade one tart after another through our bedroom, I let him rape me more times than I can remember. I watched him—the one girl my son fell in love with, they even got engaged, and that *bastard* seduced her, *bought her*, just so he could humiliate his own son. And I sat by and watched it happen, year after year, because he had broken me too." She shook her head. "But Sally Cameron? She's an even bigger bastard than he is. And she's thirty years younger than him, and she knows he needs her more than she needs him. And *she* will not tolerate the likes of Lady Bee and all the other tarts parading around the house . . ."

I said, "You think he is planning to divorce you and marry Sally?"

She looked sourly at her hands. "Of course he is. And then he'll get a taste of his own bloody medicine, because she will take him for everything he's got, and then dump him for a younger man."

Dehan shifted uncomfortably in her dress and kicked off her red satin shoes. "So, you talked to Bee, then what?"

She shrugged. "She made me angry. She couldn't see that we were both as screwed as each other. They were going to kick us both out. It made me so *mad* that all she could do was defend him . . ." She studied Dehan's face a moment. "Then you came out onto the terrace. I'm sorry about what I said." She smiled ruefully. "You're probably the first woman in years he's met and hasn't screwed."

Dehan shook her head. "So where did you go from there?"

"I went to one of the spare rooms. Frankly, I just wanted a

good cry and a sleep. As I came out into the hall . . ." She glanced at me. "You and the major and my son were just going into the study."

"How long did you stay in the guest room?"

"Until . . ." She rubbed her face with her hands and took a deep breath. "Until about half past six. Then I showered, changed, and came down."

"Did you see anybody?"

She shook her head. "No, the study door was closed."

"Who was in the drawing room?"

She shrugged. "Exactly as you saw it. You came in just after me."

"You didn't witness the row with Dr. Cameron?"

"No. He had just left when I came down. Charles was talking about it. He thought it was funny. So did Sally."

"We are almost done, Mrs. Gordon . . ."

"Please stop calling me that. I'm no' his wife anymore. I've got to stop pretending to be somebody I'm not. I'm Pamela May, no' Pamela Gordon. The only thing that tied me to that bastard was the son we had together. Now he's gone and I am free." She raised her eyes to mine. "I'm Pamela, or Pam."

I nodded. "Pam. Did Robert Armstrong have any quarrel with your son that you know of?"

She looked surprised. "Bobby?" She shrugged. "Bobby's always been a miserable bastard. Nobody likes him, except that stuck-up tart he's with, Elizabeth, Lizzie. He has always hated my . . ." She sighed. "He has always hated Charles Sr., because he says he cheated him out of his inheritance. Which is patently absurd. All he did was persuade his father not to give away their estate to complete strangers on the strength of some dubious connection based on clan history."

I shrugged. "Still, the resentment was there."

"Against Charles Sr., never against my son, as far as I am aware." She looked suddenly drawn. "Detectives, the fact is that nobody on Earth could have had any conceivable motive to kill

Charles. You knew him. That was him through and through. He was a kind, sweet, gentle soul. If anybody deserved to die it was his father, and God knows enough people had motive for that, me the first among them. It is a cruel, twisted irony that it was his son who got murdered."

There was a tap at the door and Brown stepped in. "Detectives, Dr. Cameron is here."

I looked at Dehan, we stared at each other a moment in a kind of silent telepathy, then I sighed and sat forward. "Thank you, Brown, will you send him in, please?"

He stepped out and a moment later opened the door again to admit Dr. Ian Cameron and his black bag. His face said he was both very confused and very annoyed. He took three strides, saying, "Would somebody mind telling me . . ." Then he stopped dead in his tracks, staring at Pam. After a moment, the anger drained from his face. "Pam? What in the name of God . . . ?"

I watched him approach the table, grab a chair, and drag it over beside Pamela. He held her hand, touched her face, and examined her eyes, all in a matter of a few seconds. "What happened to you, lass?" He scowled at me and Dehan. "What the hell is going on?"

Pam drew breath, but I put my hand on her arm. "Mrs. Gordon has had a very powerful, traumatic shock. You may consider she needs a sedative to be able to sleep. After that, we will tell you exactly what has happened, and in fact you may be able to help us sort it out. It's a bit of a mess."

He studied us a moment, then turned back to Pamela. "Pam?"

She nodded. "Please, Ian, just give me something to knock me out for a few hours. I'm shattered."

He opened his bag and took out a small plastic bottle of tablets. Then he looked at me. "I should accompany her . . ."

Dehan rose and went to the door. She called Brown and the major. Meanwhile, I shook my head at Cameron. "Just this once, Doc, we'll let the major and the butler do it."

"What the *hell* is going on here?"

"We're about to tell you."

The major appeared at the door. Pam took the tablets from Cameron's fingers. He said, "Take two, no more." She rose and crossed the room to the major. They departed with Cameron staring after them as Dehan closed the door. Dehan sat. Cameron looked from me to her and back again. He was worried. He repeated, "What the hell is going on? Somebody had better start explaining or else . . ."

I sat forward and interrupted him. "You had a row with Charles Gordon Sr. this evening. What was that about?"

"Mind your own fuckin' business is what it was about!"

"Was it his fucking business you were mad about?"

He stood. I don't know if he was going to leave or hit me. I looked up into his face and said, "Charles Gordon has been murdered, Doctor."

The blood drained from his face. "What? No, I . . ." He turned and pointed to the door. Then realization set in. "You mean . . ."

Dehan nodded. "The son. Charles Gordon Jr. Now, Doc, suppose we start again? What was the row about?"

FOURTEEN

HE SAT SLOWLY AT THE TABLE, STARING AT DEHAN, then at me.

"Young Charles . . . ? *Murdered?* He can't be . . . It's *absurd*! I should see the body! Thus is insane! Why, he may not even be dead! Have you all lost your minds?"

I said, "Nobody has lost their mind, Doctor, and believe me, he is not alive. We'll take you to see him in a while, so you can write a death certificate. But before that, we need to ask you some questions."

His face flushed with anger. I got the feeling that was something that happened often and easily.

"Who the bloody hell d'you think y'are? You cannot interrogate me! I'm a Scotsman in my own fuckin' country! You can't come in here demanding to ask me fuckin' questions! You bloody Americans think you can . . ."

I cut him short. "Take it easy, Doc, nobody is marching in anywhere or demanding anything. It looks like we might be cut off for the next couple of days or three. Gordon Sr. asked us to look into his son's murder. Nobody can force you to answer questions, to us or to your own cops for that matter. But he's been murdered, there is no question about that, and it makes sense to start investigating before the trail goes cold." I shrugged and spread my hands. "I can't see that it makes much difference what nationality we are. The fact is we are experienced homicide detectives." I shrugged. "But if you want to refuse to talk to us because we're Americans, that's fine, we can notify the cops when they get here that you were unwilling to cooperate."

He closed his eyes and sighed. "Don't be absurd. It's just a shock. I'm still reeling. How did it happen?"

We both stared at him for a long moment, waiting. Finally, Dehan said, "This is the third time we're having to ask you this, Doctor. We're not here for a chat and a gossip. We're here on Mr. Gordon's invitation to investigate a homicide, until such time as the Scottish PD can be notified. Now, for the third time, what did you argue about?"

He sank back in his chair. "As though you don't already know! Okay! We'll play along wuth the wee farce! Sally was—*is*—having an affair wuth that old bastard. Until recently they were at least discreet, an' I thought it would blow over. The man is notorious fer the number of women he has had affairs wuth. He seduces them, plays around with them for a week or two, then sends them packing. But that didn't happen with Sal. It went on, and on. And it just seemed to get more serious every week. 'Till suddenly we were being invited fer dinner at the fuckin' castle."

He shifted in his chair, looking around at the walls like they were making him mad. He pointed toward the drawing room again and his face flushed red. "So that he . . . so that *he* could gloat and humiliate *his wife* and *me*! *Together!* I ask you, what kind of sick bastard does that, eh?"

He half stood and sat, shifted. He couldn't keep still in his chair. "But there's more. There's more. You don't know thus. Sal's shop, that belongs to him. Mah practice, mah surgery, is above the post office, an' that belongs to him an'all. I'm thirty-seven years old. My whole practice is on his wee island. Now, what do yous think is going to happen to me if he decides he's had enough of Pamela fuckin' May because she's too old and fuckin' wrinkly? If he decides he wants *my* wife instead of his own? I'll tell yous what'll fuckin' happen. Either he'll kick me out an' force me into unemployment on the fuckin' mainland, or he'll keep me here so's him and his new fuckin' trophy bride can laugh at me and humiliate me." He stared at me for a long moment. His breathing was heavy and fast and his face was flushed. He shifted in his seat again and said savagely, "So *that's what the fuckin' row was about!*"

I scratched my chin. The wind was still moaning outside, but I was aware the thunder had grown more distant.

"What time was that?"

He shook his head. "Sal came up one thirty or two. You were there. You saw."

Dehan said, "And you?"

"I wasn't going to come. Then I thought, I can't see my patients in thus state of mind. I had to get it off my chest an' have it out with the bastard. So I come up and he were out there, in the hall, just standin' there, leering at me with his stupid face."

Dehan hid a smile behind a frown and said, "What time? It's important."

He sighed, rubbed his face, then ran his fingers through his hair. "Six, six thirty maybe."

I sat forward with my elbows on the table. "Think carefully, Doctor, where was he coming from, or going?"

He frowned at me like I was crazy. "How should I know? He was just standing there, lookin' kind o' creepy. I let 'im have it an' I left."

I raised an eyebrow. "There were no doors open to suggest where he had been or where he might be going?"

He thought about it, frowned, then shook his head. "No. Well, the cupboard, under the stairs, that was open an' the light was on. But other than that, no."

"So the study door was closed?"

He nodded. "Aye, I just told you it was. Why?"

I stared at Dehan a moment. She stared back, then turned to

Cameron with a frown. "How was your relationship with Charles Jr.?"

He shrugged, then shook his head. "You're no' going ta pin his murder on me. There was no *relationship* to speak of. We nodded to each other in the street. I never treated him as a patient. The few times we exchanged words he struck me as nice enough. To be honest I thought he was a stuck-up English prick, but he hid it under a veneer of polite deference. But then I don't like the English very much." He paused, with an aggressive challenge in his eyes. "Come to think of it, he was no' English, he was American, but I don't like Americans very much either."

Dehan sighed. "I'm sure there will be a lot of weeping in the streets of England and the USA when that bombshell gets out on Twitter, Dr. Cameron, but personally I don't give a rat's ass because I think the stuck-up prick is not the dead man you're about to see in the study, but you. But here's the thing I'm curious about, Doc, how did you get hold of the gun?"

He squinted at her like she was insane. "*What?*"

Dehan laughed and I smiled and sat back. She spread her hands. "Come on! How stupid do you think we are? More to the point, how smart do you need to be to work it out?"

"What're you talking about?"

"How did it happen? He showed Sally his revolver one day and she told you about it? She told you he kept it in a drawer in his bedroom?"

"You're insane."

"Then, when the affair got out of hand and you saw your marriage, your livelihood, and your future going down the can, you decided the old man had to go. After all, if Charles Jr. inherited, he was easy to handle, even if he *was* a stuck-up English prick. At least he wasn't screwing half the women on the island, including your wife, right? He wasn't a threat."

"Fer the last time, I don' know what you're talking about! Yous said it was Charles Jr. who was killed, not Charles Sr.! So what are you *on* about?"

She nodded. "Sure. You came into the hall. You saw Gordon Sr. outside the study in the hall and you assumed that was where he was going. So you let him have it, then went down to the kitchen. The staff were upstairs preparing the dining room for dinner. You slipped through, up the service stairs and into his bedroom where you found the revolver. Then you went down and out again. Through the window you saw the man you thought was Gordon Sr. sitting at his desk and you shot him. But you made a mistake. It was his son."

He gaped at us. "You must be absolutely fuckin' stupid, even by American standards. That is the biggest load of bollocks I have ever had the misfortune to listen to. It is laughable."

I agreed, and I was pretty sure Dehan did too, but it was interesting to see which way he jumped when he was accused.

I sat forward. "It is not so laughable, Doctor. Leave aside the details for now, you have a powerful motive to want Gordon Sr. dead, and father and son are similar enough to be mistaken through a leaded window or in poor light. You were here, outside the study at about the time of death, and you were in an altered, enraged state of mind. Add to that the fact that the storm kept knocking out the lights, I'd put you right at the top of my list of suspects, and however stupid you think Americans may be, I'm pretty sure your Scottish police will think the same way."

He flopped back in his chair and covered his face with his hands. "Jesus fuckin' Christ!"

I stood. "I want you to have a look at the body."

"Why? Is this some kind of fuckin' trap again?"

I shook my head. "No. You're a doctor. You're the only damn doctor we have, so you need to make out the death certificate."

"So am I a bloody suspect or no'?"

"Of course you are, along with just about everybody else in this house."

"Uxcept yous."

"Yeah, except us. Let's go."

We made our way through the silent, watching faces in the

drawing room and into the hallway. He stood staring, incredulous, at the broken door as I undid the padlock, and we stepped inside the room.

I watched his face carefully as he took in the scene, the wound to the head, the fallen arm, the weapon on the floor. He turned suddenly and looked at the windows, seeing they were locked.

"Thus," he said, "thus is the same . . ."

I nodded.

He shook his head. "How could I—how could anybody? That was suicide . . ."

I shook my head. "No, Doctor, it's not. Because when they examine the gun, even though they will find his prints on it, they will find no gunshot residue on his hand or his sleeve, just as in the first case." I pointed at Charles Gordon Jr.'s head. "The entry wound shows no sign of singeing from a contact shot. The trajectory of the bullet, even from a cursory examination, is clearly at a forty-five-degree angle and must have been fired from over by the fireplace. All of these facts are identical to the old man's case. So, even if you accept, which I do not, that the original case was a freak occurrence, the odds against it happening twice, in the same family, in the same house in the same room, are so astronomical as to be impossible. All of which adds up to one thing. This was a murder, staged to look the same as his grandfather's, and that means whoever did this knows how the old man was killed."

He stared at me wide-eyed. "Dear God . . ." Then his face creased into disbelief again. "But *why*? I mean, he was a twat, but he was a nice guy. There was no harm in 'im. You wouldn't want to *kill* him!"

A sudden thought made him point at me and then at Dehan. "An' your notion that I shot him through the window, by mistake, is just plain *stupid*! He was clearly shot from one o' them chairs, an' at that distance there is no mistaking the son fer the father!"

"I know."

"What?"

"We just wanted to know which way you jumped."

"You bastards!"

"You'd better believe it."

"I'm a doctor! Ah don't fuckin' kill people."

Dehan snorted. "I don't believe that's a defense at law, even in Scotland."

He sighed and seemed to sag. Then he hunkered down and opened his black bag. From it he took a form and, after a brief examination of the body, made out the death certificate. After a moment he looked up at me. "Time of death?"

I shrugged and looked at Dehan. She said, "Sometime between . . . You, me, and the major were the last people to see him alive, and that was, what, shortly before six?"

I nodded. "And Armstrong found him at shortly before eight. So that's your time of death. Where were you at that time?"

He scribbled on the form. "You know where I was. I was on my way here, I was shouting at Gordon Sr., and I was on my way home, while my wife stayed behind to play house with the Laird."

"It's not a great alibi."

"Yeah, well, if I'd known ah was goin' to need one, I'd of prepared a better one." He stood. "I'm no' stupid. If I was goin' to kill him, I wouldn'a stood shoutin' at him in the bloody hall. Besides . . ." He shook his head. "Whoever killed him intended to kill the son, no' the father. There was no mistaken identity here. Whoever killed him was sitting in one of them chairs, lookin' at him. How they got out, tha's the mystery."

"Do you mind sticking around for a while?"

"What for?"

"Pamela might need you. Also, I'd like to have you around until I've finished asking all my questions."

He sighed, then nodded. "Fine, but I'm warnin' you. If that bastard starts on at me . . ."

I interrupted him. "Don't say or do anything you're likely to regret, Doctor. There has already been one tragedy tonight. Let's try and avoid another."

He left the room and crossed into the drawing room, closing the door behind him. I stood staring at the two chairs while Dehan stared at the body. She said suddenly, "He has no motive." Then she shrugged. "Fact is, nobody has a motive. He said it himself, why would anybody want to kill him? He was just a sweet, bumbling, inoffensive guy." She looked at me for confirmation that I agreed and I nodded absently. "Plus," she went on. "How old is this killer? Let's say he or she was twenty back when they killed Old Man Gordon. That makes him or her sixty now, which narrows the field right down—to his mother, his father, and Bee. Or the major! None of them is credible, Stone."

"Mhm."

"And then there's opportunity. How the hell do we establish opportunity when we have no idea how the crime was committed?" She gestured at the two Chesterfields with both hands. "He is sitting in one of those two chairs. If he is right-handed, logic dictates it is the chair on our left, over there, which gives the correct angle and trajectory for the shot. But apparently this shooter is invisible, because Old Man Gordon was peacefully reading his book and didn't notice the guy sitting in his Chesterfield aiming a gun at his head; and Charles Jr. was, what, doing his accounts? He didn't see the guy holding his father's Smith and Wesson either. And after the invisible man or woman with the gun had shot them both, he just beamed up to the Enterprise, like he had never been here. How the hell do we establish opportunity when it is impossible to show *how* the killer was even here?"

I blinked at her, then smiled. "That's the clever bit about this whole crime, Dehan. The killer never was here."

FIFTEEN

We switched off the light, locked the study, and made our way back to the drawing room. As we entered, Bee stood and came toward us with her left hand over her heart and her right hand reaching out for me.

"Carmen, Stone, Detectives, forgive me, but I am not as young as I once was, this has all been a frightful strain on me, you have seen Pamela and Dr. Cameron, could you not take my statement now, and let me get some rest? Perhaps the doctor could give me something . . ."

"Of course, Bee." I smiled and gestured toward the dining room door.

Behind me I heard Sally's voice, harsh and a little shrill. "How long is this farce going to take?"

I turned. Gordon was frowning up at her. Everybody had turned and was watching her. Her pale skin flushed and she looked suddenly embarrassed. I said, "Farce, Mrs. Cameron?"

She glanced around. "We're all exhausted. It's been a terrible shock . . ."

"Not least for Charles Jr. and his parents. What part of this, exactly, do you see as a farce, Mrs. Cameron?"

She bridled and straightened her back where she was sitting on the arm of Gordon's chair. He muttered something to her.

She drew breath to speak but I interrupted her. "We'll be talking to you in good time, but given where you're sitting right now, I'd be cautious about using words like farce, if I were you."

She went bright red, which didn't suit the color of her hair, and I turned and followed Bee and Dehan into the dining room. I closed the door and Bee dropped into a chair, removed her hat, and placed both hands over her heart.

"Look here," she said, then looked at me and Dehan in turn. "I know you Americans are frightfully puritanical and you still believe in the flat Earth and that there were no dinosaurs and all that, but, well, you know, it isn't really *like* that!"

I burst out laughing.

Dehan's eyebrows shot up. "You are kidding me, right, Bee?"

I sat, smiling, and said, "Why don't you tell us what it *is* like, Lady Jane?"

She reached over and put her hand on my arm. "You have the benefit of Hollywood over there, and your huge television networks, that tell you all how life *should* be, *ideally*, and I think that is just *super*. But over here, you know, it's all a bit more *primal*."

Dehan shook her head and sighed. "Things get pretty primal in the Bronx, Bee. Believe me."

I gave her a gentle kick under the table and she sighed again.

Bee sat back. "I am quite sure they do, my dear. But that is a different kind of primal. That's all about fighting and killing and being badass and frightfully macho. This here . . ." She gave her head a little shake. "It's *all* about sex." She studied Dehan's face a moment, then repeated, "Sex, sex, sex, morning, noon, and night, nothing but sex. It is *quite* exhausting."

I nodded. "It would be."

"And it's no good moralizing about it. I am quite certain that if there were a god, He, She, or It would not have the faintest interest in who was tupping whom, where, how, or why. But as

He, She, or It is merely a figment of our imagination, the issue really doesn't arise, does it?"

I shook my head. "No. But perhaps you could put a little flesh on the bones for us. In what way, precisely, is Charles Jr.'s death about sex?"

"Well . . ." She folded her hands carefully on the table in front of her. "Have you ever heard of the Pitcairn Islands?"

"That is where the crew of the *Bounty* wound up, if I am not mistaken."

"Precisely. And because they were all living on a small island, they had no religion, and they all lived in somewhat primal conditions, they all became obsessed with sex. And precisely the same thing has happened here, on Gordon's Swona."

I tried not to sigh. "That is a very interesting perspective, Bee, but again, socioeconomic dynamics aside. How, precisely, docs this relate to Junior?"

"Well, I mean to say, I should have thought it was obvious!" She leaned across the table toward Dehan. "Do *you* think that if Charles Sr. were not so rich he would be half so attractive? Of course his arrogance and his stature have a certain appeal, on a very basic, animal level, but it's his *stature*, his *wealth*, the fact that he owns an island and a castle. It all adds up to sex appeal. Without the trappings he would just be obnoxious, and I speak as a woman who has adored him for decades."

Dehan had adopted a rictus that involved thin lips and narrowed eyes. I examined the walls a moment and finally said, "I am still not seeing it, Bee. Charles Jr.? Connection?"

She heaved a big sigh.

"Well, for goodness' sake . . . ! Young Charles was not *un*attractive? And aside from his father, he *was* the richest man on the island and destined to inherit everything. He was far too much of a gentleman to kiss and tell, of course, but anyone who thinks that he wasn't getting his end away is sadly misguided. I mean, a rich, personable bachelor . . ."

Dehan frowned and grunted. I was about to ask her to be more precise but she went right ahead and did just that.

"Now, I should imagine that you have been struggling, amongst other things, with the question, who *on Earth* would want to hurt such a charming, agreeable, harmless chap as Charles? Well, the answer is quite simple. Sex. Sex, to paraphrase the Bard, doth make monsters of us all. So the question becomes not who would want to harm Charles, but who was *jealous* of Charles, and hence, who was Charles getting his end away with?"

I waited, watching her. She waited, watching me back. Finally I said, "So who *was* he getting his end away with?"

"You mean *aside* from the maids?"

"Yes, Bee, aside from the maids."

"I'm sure I don't know. But if I were ten years younger, I can assure you *I'd* have had him by now. And I'm sure I'm not alone in feeling that way."

I scratched my head. "This is just speculation, Bee. Do you know, for a fact, that he was in a relationship with somebody?"

She shook her head. "But believe me, he was. And if you'll forgive the crudeness, the screw pool is not exactly vast on this island, is it?"

Dehan sighed, and there was a hint of disappointment in her voice. "Bee, where were you between six and seven this evening?"

Bee beamed. "*Darling!* Am I a suspect? How exciting! Let me see. You and I spoke on the terrace. Then you went off with Stone, such a strong name, and poor Charles and the major. I stayed in the drawing room and read a magazine, and after that the major came and joined me, we chatted. Then Charles Sr. came in with Sally, and that's about it, really."

Dehan frowned. "He came in with Sally?"

"Yes, dear."

"You heard the doctor shouting at him?"

"Oh yes, one could hardly fail to, but that was a little earlier. I'm afraid I'm not awfully good when it comes to time. One moment flows, as it were, into another."

I nodded a few times, considering the fact that there are few things in this world as slippery as a member of the British upper classes.

"In your opinion, Bee—and please understand I am only asking for your opinion—who stands to gain from Charles Jr.'s death?"

Her eyebrows arched. "Well, Pamela, naturally, and me. But only if Daddy Charles doesn't marry again, and only when he dies. Pamela will get everything. She is now, to all intents and purposes, his sole heir. I get a percentage of his estate, I don't know how much, but I believe it is generous. However . . ." She shook her head. "All of that could change overnight if he gives Pamela the old heave-ho and marries Sally. Then we are all well and truly screwed. Metaphorically. The only one who's getting screwed literally is Sally, lucky bitch."

Dehan smiled. "Bee?"

"Yes, darling?"

"Screwed *is* a metaphor. Sally is not *literally* getting screwed."

Bee smiled vacantly. "Oh, yes."

I took a deep breath. "Is there anything else, Bee, that you feel you need to tell us, or that we ought to know?"

"Not really. I am sure you are doing a simply marvelous job. I should now like to go to bed. It has been an awfully trying day. And perhaps you could ask that appalling Dr. Cameron to give me something." She stood and added absently, "They do let almost anyone into the professions these days. It is too bad, really."

Dehan went to the door with her, smiling and muttering, "No standards . . ."

"None, darling. None at all."

Bee left, and Dehan closed the door and leaned against it, looking at me. She smiled unhappily. "Some honeymoon."

I nodded, then shook my head. "Next time, I choose the destination."

"Next time?"

"You better believe it."

She gave a small laugh. "I'd like to talk to Gordon. I'd like to know about his will. He's the key to all this. Him and his dead father."

"I agree. But before we do, I'd like to have a chat with the major."

She frowned. "The major? You like him for this?"

"No, but he is the country manor equivalent of the village gossip. Whatever Bee is hinting at, he has the dope. When we talk to Gordon, I'd like to have the major's intel behind me."

She nodded. "See? That's why you're the oldest."

She turned, opened the door, and leaned out. "Major, could we have a chat?"

There was the sound of anxious bumbling closely followed by the major smiling apologetically as he hurried in. I gestured him to a chair at the head of the table and he sat. We sat on either side of him and he said, "I suppose you'll want to know what I was up to between six and eight."

I nodded. "Amongst other things."

"Of course, we were all in the study together, and he was alive at that time."

Dehan smiled. "We would have noticed if he wasn't."

He nodded, frowning. "Oh, most assuredly. No, he was definitely alive then. And after that, well, you chaps went upstairs, Charles stayed in the study, and I went over to the drawing room, hoping for a snifter."

"Was there anybody there when you went in?"

"Yes. Bee was there, reading one of those awful magazines. Offered her a drink and she said, 'Not half, gove'nor!'" He laughed out loud, then flushed bright red. "Like a Cockney, you know. She's a great laugh, old Bee. Aristocracy, you know. Never guess, not toffee-nosed at all. Just an average gal."

Dehan nodded. "Yup. Just one of the guys. So, did either of you leave the room after that?"

"Well, um, ah . . . I may have um . . . ahh . . . you know . . . um . . ."

I drummed my fingers on the table a few times. "Gone to the bathroom, Major?"

"Quite so, exactly, um, yes."

"And Bee?"

"Yuh, also, perhaps. But other than that, we were there until everyone started coming in for cocktails. Including your, uh, good selves."

"Did you see or hear anybody else during that time?"

"No, only Cameron, making a bit of a spectacle of himself, shouting at Charles. Can't blame the man, I suppose, bit of a rough deal, when you . . . when you think about it . . ." He looked embarrassed and turned away.

I leaned forward. "What is a rough deal, Major?"

He seemed to bark, like a Scottish Terrier. "Well! One doesn't like to gossip . . . man's private life . . . but, you know . . ."

"I agree, but given that this is a murder inquiry, and that our personal interest in the doctor's private life is somewhat less than zero, I think you are justified in telling us what the rough deal is."

He looked momentarily startled, then nodded. "Yes, I see, quite so, quite so. Um, well, the odd thing is that Bee and I had, just before the shouting started, you understand, had been, as it were, discussing, not gossiping but discussing, more widely, the doctor's position on the island."

I raised my eyebrows. "Really? And what did you judge his position to be?"

"Well . . . um . . ." He nodded several times. "Precarious, to say the least."

Dehan sighed noisily, like a person putting together a five-thousand-piece jigsaw puzzle, blindfolded. "Would you please explain why you thought that, Major?"

"Of course. The thing is, he was only aware of half of his problems, which is ironic, considering how things turned out. You see . . ." He leaned forward, glancing at us in turn with only his eyes. "She wasn't only seeing Charles Sr. She was also seeing Charles Jr. on the side."

"When you say seeing . . ."

"Oh, I mean that they were having a . . . you know . . . carnal affair, not to put too fine a point on it. Bit of the old one-two, if you follow."

Dehan raised an eyebrow. "And you are sure of this?"

"Oh, absolutely. No shadow of a doubt."

"How can you be so sure?"

"Well, he told me."

Dehan looked skeptical. "Kiss and tell? That doesn't sound like Jr."

"No! Quite so. You are absolutely right, but you see, I was a bit of a confidant for the poor boy. Bee and I have sort of been around all his life, and he could never really confide in his father, or poor Pam for that matter, so Bee and I sort of stepped into the breach, if you follow. The poor boy wasn't bragging about a conquest; far from it, he was worried sick about what would happen if his father found out."

I said, "Let me see if I have this straight, Major. You are telling us that Sally Cameron was not only having an affair with Charles Gordon Sr., but also with his son, at the same time."

"Devil of a thing, hey? Well, I didn't know what to tell the poor chap. I mean, I am a man of the world in that I have traveled just about everywhere on the globe, but tended to keep my nose clean where women were concerned, if you follow."

My mind reeled for a moment at the choice of metaphor, but I tried to ignore it and thought about this new angle. The major kept talking.

"Of course, he didn't go looking for it. He never did. But from what he told me, she sought him out."

Dehan was observing him through narrowed eyes. "How?"

The major suppressed a schoolboy laugh. "Went to his room while the old man was snoring! Spirited girl, but a bit naughty."

"So he came to you to discuss this because he was worried."

"Yes. Well, he would be, wouldn't he?"

"What was it, exactly, that he was worried about?" Before he could answer, she preempted him. "I mean, Major, I can see that there are several aspects to that situation that would be worrying, but what I am asking you is, precisely, what was the thing that was worrying him the most?"

He stared at her for a moment, like he was replaying her question in his head. Then he blinked and said, "Well, what his father would do if he found out. I mean, Charles Sr. is, um . . ."

He hesitated, so I said, "A cruel, vindictive man?"

He held my eye for a long moment, then said, "Yes. Yes, precisely that. A cruel, vindictive man."

SIXTEEN

Dehan pushed the door closed after the major. We were alone in the silent dining room. She stood facing the closed door a moment and then turned and started pacing slowly around the room in her red scarlet dress and bare feet, with her fingers laced behind her neck.

"The more information we get," she said, "the further we are from an answer. We need some kind of fixed point: something we can say, 'This is a cert!' So I am going to say for now that Pam did not kill her son. With this crowd of crazies you can't be sure, Stone . . ." She stopped walking and turned to face me, with her fingers still laced behind her head. She seemed to be very far away, at the other end of the long table. "But for now I am going to take that as a fixed point. Okay?"

I nodded. "Okay."

She turned and carried on walking. "So, who had motive? Bee seems to have no apparent motive, and on the face of it, neither does the major. Agreed?"

"Agreed."

She reached the end of the room and started pacing back. "Armstrong has reason to hate Gordon Sr., but other than hating the whole Gordon family, seems to have no special grudge against

Jr." She stopped, eyed me a moment. "Dr. Cameron, on the other hand, has a very powerful motive."

"He has?"

She started walking again. "Sure. Relations between Sally and the doc are strained to breaking point. She is ready to give him his marching orders. They are bad enough that they are having rows in public, and where before she was just having an affair on the side, now she is seriously thinking of giving Ian the boot. They row and out of sheer spite she tells him, not only is she screwing the old man, she's getting her leg over with Junior too."

"I am horrified at your language, Dehan. I should never have brought you to this primal place."

"More than that, how about this? Her plan is not to force a divorce between Gordon Sr. and Pam, it is to marry Gordon Jr. and become part of the family."

I shook my head. "Mmmnyahh . . ."

"Mnyah why?"

"If she is hitting the hay with Dad, she cannot possibly expect to be welcomed into the family with open arms by him if she then declares she intends to marry his son."

She extended her left arm and pointed her finger at me like a gun. "Wrong, Stone, if she intended to *continue* sleeping with Dad after the marriage. That level of humiliation would have been right up Gordon Sr.'s street. But either way, if she was planning to marry Junior and told Cameron about it, that gives him a motive, which he did not have before."

"Granted."

"And we know he was in the area at the time, and he has no alibi."

"Also granted."

She stopped walking and put both hands on the back of the chair opposite me. "Now, let's get a little darker: Gordon Sr. likes to dish it out, but he doesn't look to me like the kind of man who likes to take it. So, while he thinks it's a gas to humiliate his son by seducing his fiancée, when his son hits the sack with the woman he is planning to marry, I figure that could make him real mad. Mad enough to kill."

I nodded. "It's possible."

"It's more than possible. And note where he was when Cameron came in and started shouting at him. Right outside the study, where his son was locked in, doing his accounts, within the window for the time of death."

I did a lot of nodding, then said, "All good, solid reasoning."

"But?"

"No buts, just two questions: One, how did he do it? And two, what is the connection between this murder and the murder of his grandfather forty years ago?"

"Same answer to both." She spread her hands. "I don't know."

I stood. "Let's get him in here and ask him."

I went to the door, opened it, and leaned out.

"Mr. Gordon, could we talk to you for a moment?"

He stared at me, like an ancient, giant Nordic king. Beside him, still sitting on the arm of his chair, was Sally, watching me with hard, calculating eyes. I wondered for a moment at the woman who had been sleeping with the man who sat dead across the hall with half his head blown away, yet showing no emotion on her face but caution. She held my eye a moment, then Gordon stood, sighed, and strode unsteadily across the room to join me.

Dehan closed the door as he grunted and lowered himself into the chair at the head of the table. "Couldn't some of this have waited till the morning? Sally is exhausted, and frankly, so am I."

"No."

I sat. Dehan remained standing, leaning against the wall. He looked at her sourly, then turned away.

"I need to know everything about your relationship with Sally Cameron."

He didn't look at me. He just stared sullenly at the table. "Go to hell."

"I can't hold a gun to your head, Mr. Gordon. I can't even

point one at you from the fireplace. It's your choice. But what I can and will do is inform the cops when they get here that after asking me to investigate, as soon as we touched on the subject of your affair with Sally Cameron, you clammed up and told me to go to hell. If you want to draw attention to your affair, that is certainly the way to do it."

He grunted again and was then silent for a while. Finally, he said, "It's not relevant."

I shook my head. "No. I decide that. Or you can go to hell and get somebody else to investigate."

He fiddled with his thumbs for a bit, then said, "Fine. So I'm screwing Sally. So what?"

I turned to Dehan. "Let's go pack and get some sleep. We'll catch the first ferry once the storm stops and make a statement at the police station at John o'Groats."

"Okay!" He snarled it at the tabletop.

I leaned down and put my face close to his. "Listen to me, Gordon. You are not doing me a favor. I'm doing you one, you understand? All I want is to have my honeymoon with my wife. Now, if you want me to get your sorry ass out of this mess, you had better come clean and tell me what the hell is going on, because I *do not* intend to get prosecuted by the British cops for concealing or suppressing evidence. So if you want my help, start talking. I want to know *everything* about your relationship with Sally Cameron."

He watched me carefully.

I sat. "And just remember, I have been talking to other people who have been watching and observing you both. I'll know if you hold back." I pointed at the door. "And one more attempt to bull-shit me, and me and my wife go through that door."

He heaved another big sigh.

"Things have not been good between me and Pamela for some time."

Dehan snapped, "Try forty years."

He glanced at her, but other than that, showed no sign of

having heard. "After my father died I discovered . . . somebody told me . . . that Pamela had been my father's lover. It embittered me. She was already pregnant with my son . . ."

He faltered.

I stared at him. "Son of a gun," I said. "You don't know, do you? You were never sure, and you couldn't bring yourself to do the paternity test. It probably wouldn't have been conclusive anyway. So instead you spent his whole life abusing and humiliating him for his mother and your father's sins."

He didn't answer. He stared at the wall across the room for a long moment, then blinked and looked back at his thumbs. "When the boy was born, I raised him as my own, though he may well have been my half brother, as well as my stepson. It was nauseating. I began to have affairs. Whether Pamela did or not, I neither know nor care. And yes." He looked at me with hard, resentful eyes. "On the rare occasions when Charles entered into a sentimental relationship with some insipid female, I would make a point of seducing her. It was my small act of vengeance against my father and my wife."

He stood, crossed the room to the sideboard, and poured himself a large whiskey. He sipped it and spoke without turning.

"But all that changed when I met Sally. I can honestly say that every relationship I have had since Pamela has been an act of cruelty and revenge." Now he turned, glanced at Dehan, and then looked at me, as though he expected me to understand. "Sally was different. With Sally—it may sound adolescent and naïve—but with Sally I began to heal. I began to believe that it is possible to love and trust. She is not like other women."

"You fell in love with her."

He looked sullen and his face darkened. "You can mock if you want."

"I'm not mocking, Gordon. The only bitter cynic in this room is you. So you fell in love, good for you. What else?"

He frowned at me. "Nothing else. We had discussed it and

agreed that she would tell Ian and I would tell Pam, then we would both divorce our spouses and marry."

I scanned his face and he scanned mine back. He looked like he was trying to understand what I was getting at. If it was an act, it was a good one. I said, "Where did that leave Pam and Ian?"

He shrugged. "Pam would get alimony and some kind of settlement, and Ian would continue as doctor in the village. I think the man is an insufferable prig, but I harbor no ill will toward him. I have no desire to see him bankrupt or broken."

I waited a moment, watching him carefully. Then I asked, "Was Sally seeing anybody else?"

He looked startled, then laughed. "Don't be ridiculous. I just told you we were going to get married."

"Like your son and his fiancée?"

He scowled at me. "What's your point?"

"That just because people are engaged to be married, it doesn't mean they don't screw around."

"Sally is not like that."

"So she wasn't screwing your son?"

He threw back his head and roared with laughter. "That's your theory?" He laughed again. "You're clutching at straws." He gestured at me, then at Dehan. "This? This is New York's finest? Give me a break!"

I glanced at Dehan. She shrugged with her eyebrows. I sat back in my chair. "Just a couple more questions."

"I hope they're a bit more intelligent than the last one, Detective Stone."

"What were you doing in the broom cupboard?"

He went very still. "What?"

"When Cameron turned up to tell you what he thought of you, you had been doing something in the broom cupboard. What?"

He didn't answer for a very long moment. Then he looked up at me and narrowed his eyes. "If you must know, Brown told me you had asked to look inside. I was curious to see what you had been looking for."

"Isn't it obvious?"

"Yes, of course, some kind of secret door. I wondered if you had found one, but on inspecting all those shelves, as you must have done, it was clear there was no secret door there." He sighed again. "Anything else, Stone?"

I nodded. "Yeah."

"What? I am beginning to think I would have been better off allowing chaos and mayhem to reign. At least I might have got some sleep."

"Tell me about your will."

"*My* will?"

The answer surprised me, as did the expression on his face. It was hard to fathom. "Yes, Mr. Gordon, your will. Who else's will would I be asking you about?"

He made a face, shrugged, shook his head. "It might make sense to ask about Charles' will. After all, *he* is the one who has been murdered. I would have thought the pertinent question would be who benefits from *his* death, not mine."

"I was under the impression," I said, "that he had no wealth of his own. That your wealth would one day be his wealth."

He shrugged again. "I have no idea what he had. I really wasn't interested. I let him use the castle as an hotel. He made something from that. It entertained me to have guests."

"Was he your heir?"

"For the moment, yes. Him and Pam. But obviously, in view of my upcoming marriage to Sally, it was in my mind to change my will. I hadn't decided on the details yet."

"Is Bee a beneficiary?"

"She receives something. Why? Why these questions about my will?"

I stood, stretched my back, and heard the vertebrae crack. I took a few paces away, staring unseeing at the room around me. I was aware of something nagging at my mind, but each time I tried to grasp it, it dispersed like mist. Then I heard myself ask, as though the question had come from somewhere else, "What, exactly, *is* your fortune, Mr. Gordon?"

"What is this impertinence?"

I turned to face him. He was scowling at me.

"It's a very simple question. What is your fortune? What do you own? This castle? The island? Is there more in Boston? Mainland Britain? What about stocks and shares? What is your income? How rich are you, and what is the nature of your wealth?"

He stood. "You're going too damned far, Stone! I said I'd pay you anything you ask to clear up Charles' murder, not to go prying into my private, personal affairs! It's none of your damned business what my fortune is or what I'm worth!"

I shrugged. "Suit yourself. Either way, I know who killed your son, and your father. And I know how."

Dehan stared at me wide-eyed, mirroring Gordon's face across the table. His eyes bulged and so did his cheeks, erupting in a sudden expostulation, "You're bluffing!"

I shook my head. "Makes no difference to me. Sounds like the storm is easing off. Tomorrow or the day after, we'll be on our way to enjoy the rest of our honeymoon somewhere a little less remote and stressful. And you can sit there and tell the Scottish police to go to hell. But I guarantee, they will be asking the very same questions as me. You know why? Because I will have put them into their heads before I leave."

He sneered at me, but without much conviction. "Forty years people have been trying to solve that murder, and now you're going to come along and . . ."

I smiled. "It's what we do." I turned to Dehan. "Come on, Dehan, let's go get some sleep."

"Wait!" He became serious. "You really know who killed my son, and my father?"

I nodded. "Yes. I know who and I know how."

"And you can prove it?"

I sighed. "If you help me, yes."

"Tell me who, and how!"

I shook my head. "We do it my way. First you tell me about your money . . ."

He sighed, rubbed his face, and said, "Fine, I'll have to contact my solicitor when the storm blows over, to bring . . . everything. He'll have to come over . . ."

"How long will that take?"

"Not long, he's just over the water. You'll have to know . . . the details . . . I suppose." He stared at me hard. "But I am counting on you to keep this *strictly* confidential! *That's* the deal!"

SEVENTEEN

Sally stood, but the others remained seated. They all stared. Then Sally half rushed across the room, staring at Gordon with anxious eyes, saying, "Oh, Charles! Come and sit down. What you must be going through!"

She led him back across the room to a chair and sat him down. I glanced at Ian. There was real hatred in his eyes as he watched them. I took a deep breath and spoke.

"We're pretty much done here."

Armstrong looked offended. "Ye haven't spoke t'me! Ye haven't got mah point of view!"

I nodded at him. "That's because I don't need it, Armstrong." I looked back at the others. "We now have statements from everybody who was at the house at the time of Charles' murder. We hope to be able to contact the police on the mainland tomorrow, and they can take over from there." I smiled at Dehan. "And we can get back to our honeymoon." I looked back at the assembled faces. "I should tell you, however, that we *have* been able to establish who murdered Charles tonight, who murdered his grandfather almost forty years ago, and how it was done."

There was a collective gasp from those assembled except

Cameron, to my right and slightly behind me, who looked at me with contempt and sneered, "You have got to be kidding!"

I ignored him and watched the major get unsteadily to his feet. He was frowning hard. He spoke above a rising murmur of voices. "Are you *serious*? But . . ." He shook his head. "That's fantastic. I hope you're not . . . How could you possibly . . . ?"

Armstrong, sitting beside Cameron, raised his voice above the others. "He couldn't, tha's how! Ut's no' possible. He's bluffing!"

Sally was speaking urgently to Gordon. Gordon was shaking his head, answering under his breath. Cameron was on his feet, approaching me. "If you know who done it, tell us! I say ye're full o' bullshit!"

Armstrong stayed seated, half shouting. "Yiz don't know shit!"

If you shout back, they just shout louder. So I spoke quietly. "I will communicate my findings to the police tomorrow, and they will act on them and it will be up to them to find the evidence to prove, or disprove, what Detective Dehan and I have found." The room fell silent. I added, "You all had the opportunity to speak before. If you have anything to say, that was the time to have said it. If you didn't say it then, I suggest you wait till morning and tell the cops when they arrive."

Armstrong spoke up again. "Ah didneh get a chance to speak. You don't want ta hear what ah have to say, do ye? Wha's the matter? The old man paying yous to keep a few things quiet?"

Suddenly Sally was on her feet and Gordon was pulling at her arm, telling her to sit and be quiet. But she wasn't in the mood to sit or be quiet. Her red hair flying and her blue eyes flashing, she let rip.

"*Why don't you shut yer fuckin' mouth, Bobby Armstrong? All you and yer bloody whooring mother ever did was cause trouble! Why don't you fuckin' sit doon an' shut yer fuckin' trap fer once in your fuckin' life!*"

You have never really seen anger until you have seen an angry Scotsman. Armstrong's face went crimson and the veins in his forehead stood out and pulsed. His eyes were wide and staring. He stood and his voice was a rasp in his throat.

"*Who are you callin' a fuckin' whoore? Fuckin' thus thievin' bastard and fuckin' his son at the same fuckin' time! An' you call my mother a whoore?*"

I saw Gordon flash a look at Sally and then at me. He was putting two and two together. But Armstrong hadn't finished yet. He was stabbing the air with a finger that would have pierced concrete.

"*At least mah mother was faithful te Old Gordon. At least she loved the old man! But you? You are just a gold digging fuckin' user!*" He turned and pointed at Cameron. "*Ye're married to a good man! An honest man! And you humiliate him every fuckin' day with yer filthy, disgusting behavior! Ye should be ashamed o'yerself!*"

Sally was not about to be silenced. "*Och! Spare me yer bloody moralizing sermon, you hypocritical piece o'shite! You think we don't know what you do when you get the ferry across to John o'Groats? You think the whole island doesn't know you been seeing whoores? Cause no fuckin' island woman will touch you!*"

Armstrong went dangerously quiet. "What I been doin' in John o'Groats is my own buznezz, Sally Cameron. But I'll tell you thus. The only person on this island who doesn't know about you and tha' dead man in there, is his thievin' fuckin' father."

The room was deathly silent. The major was staring hard at the floor. Sally had gone very pale. Armstrong sneered at Gordon, then turned to me. "Did yous include that titbit in your brilliant piece o'detection? Ah bet ye didn't."

He turned and sat down again. Cameron was still standing by my side, staring at Sally.

I looked around the room. "Are we all done? Good. I suggest you all go to your rooms and get some rest. Brown will arrange a couple of rooms for Mr. Armstrong and Dr. Cameron. I would ask you all to please stay tomorrow morning to speak to the police when they arrive. I am sure they will want to talk to you."

Gordon got to his feet and looked suddenly like an old, broken man. Perhaps in that moment, he understood for the first time the nature of the weapon he had been wielding most of his adult life against his family. Sally reached out for him but he waved her away and crossed the room to the door.

Somebody rang the bell for Brown, and shortly afterward, he led Cameron and Armstrong out into the hall and up the stairs to the spare rooms. That left Sally and the major. He made to leave, then stopped by the door and looked back at me. "Is it a bluff? Do you really know?"

I nodded.

He said, "Who *and* how . . . ?"

"Who and how, Major."

He turned and hurried away, across the checkerboard floor and up the stairs, muttering something about talking to Bee. Sally stood watching us. After a moment, she said, "I guess I've blown it."

Dehan nodded a few times. "Nothing like screwing a man's son to undermine trust in a relationship."

I frowned and shook my head. "What made you do it, Sally?"

She sighed, seemed to sag, and lowered herself onto the arm of the chair where Gordon had been sitting. "You live in New York, fer God's sake! How could you ever begin to understand what it's like to live on an island like thus? It's no purgatory. Purgatory is where we go fer a day out. I'm thirty years old. If I don't get out now, I never will. I'll spend the rest of my existence here, on this island."

I went over to the tray of decanters and poured three drinks. I gave one to Dehan and another to Sally. "That doesn't really answer my question. I get that you wanted to get out. I get that you and Gordon could have a marriage of convenience. I even get that if you knew he and Pamela were not happy, you'd be prepared to break them up. I don't approve, but I get it. What I don't get is why his son. Why Junior?"

She looked down into her glass for a while. "I'm no' proud of it. It was Bee. She looks dappy, but she's a smart cookie, I can tell ye. An' she's known Charles fer years. She saw what was goin' on between us right at the start, and even then she advised me no' to fall for him. She said he played with people, used them against each other, an' she told me about all the things he'd done to Pam over the years. To be honest, I felt sorry for her." She shrugged. "I mean, there was nothing I could do fer her. Their marriage was over, you know what I mean? It was over a long time before he met me. An' I was determined to get off o' the island one way or another. Cameron was fuckin' useless. He thinks you have to be faithful to your fuckin' roots an' all that shite. If I stayed wuth him, I'd be here for the rest o'my days. An' that was no' goin' to happen."

"You're losing me."

"Sorry. I . . . Bee scared me. I could see myself jumping from the bloody frying pan into the fire. Land up married to the old goat *and* stuck on this bloody island with the old bastard playin' with me and humiliating me the way he humiliates the rest of his bloody family. Or did, when he had one. So I thought . . ." She shrugged.

"You thought Charles Jr. was a better bet long term, so you'd hedge your bets and play them both. Junior was bound to come into some money at some time, and when he did, you'd jump ship."

"Something like that, aye."

"Were you aware of the terms of the old man's will?"

She avoided my eye. "I asked him a couple of times, but he refused to tell me."

I gave it a beat, then asked, "Was Charles going to tell his father?"

She looked startled. "No! He was terrified of his father. We both agreed. For now, until things . . ."

She faltered and Dehan asked, "Things what?"

She shook her head. "I don't know. Until things had settled. We were just putting off a crisis."

I smiled. "Until you were firmly married into the family money."

Her eyes were hostile. "I can't stop you from judging me, but that doesn't mean you have the right."

I never got to answer. There was a scream. It was shrill and touched with hysteria. It echoed over the banisters along the galleried landing and filled the hallway. I ran out of the drawing room and saw Bee in a pink negligee, waving her hands in the air and shouting, "*Pam! Pamela! She's done something! Oh God! Come quick! Please! Come quick!*"

I swore under my breath and sprinted up the stairs three at a time. Bee ran, her pink robe flapping behind her, leading the way to the room where Pam had been taken by Cameron. I could hear Dehan right behind me, struggling in her tight red evening dress.

By the time we got to the room, just about everybody else was there, crowding around the door. I shoved my way through and found Cameron kneeling beside Pam's bed. There was an empty pill bottle on her bedside table and an empty glass of water. I snapped, "Has anyone touched that glass or the bottle?"

Cameron snarled, "I'm losing her, I'm fuckin' losing her! *Somebody get me my case!*"

Sally ran from the room. I repeated, "Has anybody touched these things?"

Cameron flushed and shouted, "*No! Now get the fuck out of here!*"

I ignored him and turned to the door. Brown's bewildered, sleepy face had added itself to the throng along with the two girls. I said, "Brown, get me two freezer bags. Quick as you can."

He shook his head. "What . . . ?"

"Now!"

He hurried away. The major was helping Cameron get Pam to her feet. Sally came back with Cameron's case, squeezed into the room, and handed it to him. She said, "What can I do?"

He snarled, "You can get out'a my fuckin' sight, is what you can do!"

She went pale and backed away. Cameron and the major took Pam to the en suite. I heard feet running up the stairs and a moment later one of the maids appeared, breathless and wide-eyed, and handed me a roll of freezer bags. I bagged the bottle and the glass and handed them to Dehan. She grabbed them and turned to the crowd.

"Okay, guys, let's let the doc do his job."

They backed away a step or two, jostling against each other. Bee had her hands over her mouth and was blinking back tears. She kept repeating, "I just came to see if she was all right . . ." Armstrong was peering over her head with a sullen twist to his mouth.

"How do we know he didn't do ut hi'sen?"

Dehan said, "Just get out, Armstrong, and try not to talk for a while."

"Fuck yous!"

I stepped over to him. "Hey, wiseass. You know what? We're not in New York. You know what that means? It means if I smack you in that big mouth of yours, I don't lose my job. Talk to my wife like that again and I'll throw you over the damn banisters."

He was going to tell me to try but decided against it and went away muttering. I looked around. I couldn't see Gordon. I went back into the room. In the bathroom I could hear the sound of dry retching. My mind was racing. I looked at the decanter on the bedside table. In the bathroom I could hear Cameron saying, "We got to make her vomit . . . I don't know why she won't . . ."

There were more ugly, spasmodic noises. I kept staring at the decanter. It was almost full. I swore violently and went into the bathroom. They had Pam kneeling over the pan, trying to make her throw up the tablets. I stared at the soles of her feet.

I said, "She was injected."

Cameron turned and stared at me. "*What?*"

I pointed. "There. On the sole of her foot. The decanter is full. The tablets were to make it look like suicide."

Something close to panic twisted his face. "But, what the hell did he give her? How am I supposed . . . ?"

"Whatever is missing from your bag! Where the hell is Gordon?"

I turned and ran. Dehan was ahead of me with Bee by her side, shouting, "*At the end! On the left! At the end!*"

She left Bee behind. She had her red dress hiked up around her hips and was speeding down the passage on her long legs and bare feet. She angled around the corner, collided with the wall, and kept going toward the door at the end.

Behind me I could hear Sally running and screaming, "*Oh, God, no! No!*" and Bee panting close behind her. There were other voices, maybe Brown. Dehan grabbed the handle and shoved. It was not locked. She burst through and I came in just behind her. We stopped dead.

Behind me I heard a small gasp, then a short scream, followed by more short, hysterical screams.

Gordon looked shocked. He looked shocked because his eyes were bulging out of the sockets in his head. His tongue was huge and protruding and his face was bloated and had turned dark purple, like a giant, grotesquely deformed eggplant. There was blood on his dressing gown and on his pajamas, but not much, and only around the collar, where he had clawed at the dressing gown cord that was tied around his neck. The other end was tied to the frame of his four-poster bed. His toes, barely touching the mattress, were still twitching.

EIGHTEEN

WE CUT HIM DOWN, AND BETWEEN ME, DEHAN, AND Brown, we laid him out on the bed. He was dead and well beyond resuscitation. I told Brown, "Go and tell Dr. Cameron that Charles Gordon Sr. is dead, will you? Tell him to come here as soon as he can."

Brown nodded, said, "Yes, sir," and left the room. Outside, Sally was sobbing violently. She had her back against the wall and her face covered with her hands. Bee had come in and sat on a padded stool by the door, where she was just staring at the deformed monstrosity that had been the man she loved.

Dehan backed away from the bed and stood staring around at the room. She looked tired. She spread her hands. "It could be either . . ."

I shook my head. "It's not suicide."

"How can you be sure?"

I made a gesture to her to hang on a minute and turned to Bee. "Bee . . . ?" She seemed not to hear me. I approached her and hunkered down in front of her, obscuring her view of the bed. "Bee, you can't be here. It's a crime scene." I smiled. "You might be sitting on evidence. And in any case, it's not a good place for you. This isn't how you want to remember him."

She gave a small smile and nodded, then she reached for my hand and held it, staring at it. "I only held his hand once or twice, you know. So many years ago. He had strong hands, like yours. I remember it as though it were yesterday. Or this morning." She raised her eyes to mine again. "You can't do it, you know?"

"What's that, Bee?"

"Play around with love and sex. It's not a game. Sooner or later, all that passion just turns . . ." Her eyes looked past me at the obscenity on the bed, and she said simply, "Ugly."

I nodded. "If only more people understood that, Bee. Come on." I stood, pulled her gently to her feet, and guided her to the door. There she stood a moment, looking at Sally. Next thing, Sally was crossing the corridor with an ugly, twisted, crying face and her arms held out, and the two women were holding each other and sobbing into each other's shoulders.

Dehan put a hand on my shoulder. "We need to get a grip on this situation, Sensci. Where is everybody?"

I nodded. "More to the point, where *was* everybody?" I moved to the door up one and across the passage from Gordon's bedroom and tried it. It was locked. I called, "*Brown!*"

I heard the scuffle of feet and the butler came hurrying around the corner. "Dr. Cameron will be with you in a moment, sir!"

I pointed at the door. "Can you unlock this, please? And let's get everybody assembled in there."

Dehan grabbed Bee and Sally and gently propelled them toward the spare bedroom while Brown fished out his keys, opened the door, and switched on the light. I went around the dogleg and found Armstrong and the two maids leaning on the doorjamb and Cameron pushing his way between them. He caught sight of me and said, "What the hell is it now?"

I pointed at Armstrong. "You, in that room with Bee and Sally, now." He drew breath. "Give me any more of your attitude and I'll throw you in there myself."

He sighed noisily and pushed past me muttering something

about fuckin' Yankees. He went in the room with Bee and Sally and I called Brown over.

"Lock Mrs. Gordon in her room and give Dr. Cameron the key. Put one of your girls on the door, the other on the spare bedroom, tell them to raise merry hell if anybody tries to get in or out. Nobody, and I do mean nobody, goes in there but him or me and my wife. Understood?"

He nodded vigorously. "Of course, sir."

He went away to lock the door. I turned to the doctor. "Come with me. You need to write out another death certificate."

He didn't say anything until we got to the room. Then he stood on the threshold, staring at the body.

"Dear God, what happened here?"

"He was hanged. He has his own dressing gown cord tied around his neck in some kind of a slipknot." I pointed at the frame of the bed. "You can see where it was tied. We cut him down, but he was already dead."

He turned and looked at me bitterly. "I have to say, Detective Stone, you're doin' a great job of solving this crime. You know who it is and how they did it, but you're going to leave them to run around killing the rest of us till mornin'? Tha's a great plan!"

I fought down the irritation I felt and said, "I need two things from you, Doctor, and one of them is not any more of your attitude. I need a death certificate, and I need to know if there is any bruising premortem or perimortem."

He muttered something obscene in some ancient, primal Celtic language and opened his bag. Dehan came in and stood staring at me. With her hair disheveled, the strained expression on her face, the scarlet dress, and her long, tanned leg showing through the slash, the only word to describe her was ravishing. She shook her head and said, "When I bought this dress, this isn't exactly what I had in mind."

I smiled at her, but it wasn't a happy smile. "You want to go and change? I got this."

She shook her head. "Let's try and work out what happened

here. Time of death . . ." She took a deep breath and blew noisily. "Anytime after he left the drawing room and came upstairs . . ."

I turned to Cameron. "You didn't sedate Bee . . ."

He was carefully removing the rope from Gordon's neck and spoke without looking at me. "I gave her a mild sedative, but it apparently had no effect." Then he added, "I hope you're no' seriously suggesting that she is capable of . . ."

"Can it!" I turned back to Dehan. "Who else was not in the room?"

She shook her head. "Only Brown and the maids."

"So, at this stage, once everybody got upstairs and went into their rooms, it could have been anyone except Pam. So we'll need to see who can alibi whom."

She nodded. "But it does mean that whoever it was was not waiting for him in the room. They came afterwards. He was already changed, but he had his dressing gown on, so either he hadn't gone to bed or, most likely, whoever it was knocked, he put on his gown, and came to the door."

I nodded. "Then one of two things happened: either his killer overpowered him and strung him up, which seems very unlikely given Gordon's weight and strength, and . . ." I looked around. "The absence of any sign of a struggle; or they had a weapon and threatened him with it. They forced him to tie the rope, put it around his neck, and gave him a shove."

Cameron stood. "There's a third possibility yer no' considering, Stone, an' that's that his conscience got too much for him. He saw what he had done to the people around him, an' how all the fuckin' wickedness of his way of life had come back on him, an' he took his own life. Bear in mind, in one single night, he lost his son and the woman he thought loved him. No' many men could get over that."

I heard him out, then said, "It's an obvious and logical possibility, Doctor, but when we cut him down, his toes could barely reach the mattress. Which means that he was standing on something that the killer rather foolishly removed after killing him."

Cameron frowned. "Why would they do that?"

Dehan shrugged with one shoulder. "They were in a rush, in a panic. Maybe Bee had just started shouting for everyone to come. Hard to think clearly in a moment like that, especially if you are improvising. Perhaps he was afraid whatever it was would be fingerprinted, and he had no time to wipe off his prints."

I nodded. "It's possible. We're dealing with a very tight time frame." I glanced around the room. "He came up the stairs. When everybody had retired to their rooms he went in, dosed Pamela, emptied the pill bottle down the toilet, slipped out, and came 'round to Gordon's room. He knocked . . ." I trailed off and pointed at a wooden box on top of a tallboy against the wall.

I went and had a closer look. There were slight impressions of dust on the surface, but it was hard to be sure. I shrugged. "It will be interesting to see what forensics gets off this box."

I turned. Dehan was frowning. "So there's a second weapon?"

I nodded.

She shook her head. "I don't like that, Stone. It's messy. Where from? If he had a weapon, why'd he need to steal the old Smith and Wesson? Where'd he get it from? All that time when everyone was in the drawing room . . ." She shook her head again. "What? He stepped out of the drawing room and found a pistol somewhere? I don't like it."

Cameron was watching us. "Yous keep talking about a man. It could just as easily have been a woman." He pointed at Gordon. "He has no premortem or perimortem bruising. He was not physically forced to hang hi'self. Either somebody held a gun to his head or he committed suicide. An' frankly, my money is on that. Frankly, I think you're both full o'crap. It is plainly obvious what happened."

Dehan raised an eyebrow at him. "It is? Care to enlighten us?"

He pointed at Gordon. "Nobody stole his gun. He took it down hi'self. This bastard killed his son because he found out that he was shaggin' my wife, his mistress. After you told everyone you had solved the murder, he believed you, came upstairs, and in a final act of malice and rage he killed his wife and then went and hanged hi'self."

I sighed. "I just told you he couldn't reach."

"How fuckin' hard would it be tu pull hi'self up, hold on to the frame with one arm an' slip the noose around his fuckin' neck, then let go?"

"Pretty hard. Will you do me a favor?"

"What?"

"Have you got surgical gloves?"

"Of course."

"Do you buy them on the island?"

He squinted at me like he was trying to fathom the depth of my stupidity. "*What?*"

I gave him a moment, trying to hold on to my patience. "I'm not going to repeat the question, Cameron. It was very clear."

"No! I don't buy them on the fuckin' island. What kind of a fuckin' stupid question is that?"

"Have you got a pair with you?"

"In mah bag. *Why?*"

I held out my hand. He stared at it a moment, then sighed laboriously, reached in his bag, and pulled out a sealed pack with a pair of surgical gloves in it. I tore the wrapper and pulled on the gloves, then I hunkered down, pulled over his bag, and started going through it slowly and meticulously. After a moment, I said to Dehan, "You still got those freezer bags?"

"Yeah."

She stepped over. I heard a rip and she squatted down next to me holding an open bag. I held up a syringe and looked up at Cameron. "You always keep your syringes lying around in your bag out of their packaging?"

He went pale. "Never. I have no idea how that got in there . . ."

I dropped it into the improvised evidence bag and smiled at Dehan. "There's your weapon. The needle is down the can on its way to the bottom of the North Atlantic." I looked back at

Cameron. "I'm prepared to bet that if the ME looks hard enough among all the bruising caused by the rope, he'll find a needle mark on the right side of Gordon's neck."

Dehan stood. "That's why there was no syringe in Pam's bedroom. He brought it with him, knocked on the door. Threatened Gordon with it, made him climb on the bed, probably on the box, then pushed him off, and replaced the box when Bee started screaming . . ."

"He flushed the needle, made his way to Pam's room, and when the doc arrived, he dropped the syringe back in his bag. If we're lucky, we may get prints from it." I stood and looked at Cameron, who was staring at me with his mouth open. "You want to get off my case now, Doctor?"

Dehan said, "Our pool of suspects is very small, and the doc is right. It could just as easily be a woman."

I nodded. "Doc, will you leave your bag there and join the others in the spare bedroom, please?"

He was shaking his head. "Och, no, you cannot believe that I did thus . . ."

"You want to tell me why?"

He fumbled and stammered, "I might have had reason to want the old man dead, but why would I kill young Charles? An' Pam?"

Dehan shrugged. "To frame somebody else? The whole damn household heard you threaten Gordon. Your exact words were, if I remember rightly, that you would make him pay and you would destroy him. Killing his son and his wife, and then him, and making it look like he did it himself, seems to me to be a pretty comprehensive way of destroying him, Doc." She nodded at his bag. "And you own the weapon."

His face cleared. "I was with Brown! He'll tell yous. I was with him!"

"When?"

"When . . ." He faltered.

I shook my head. "It's a very small window, Doc, but we don't know exactly when he was killed. Hold on to that thought. And my advice, for now, keep your mouth shut. You'll do everyone a favor. Now, please, leave the bag there and get into the spare bedroom with the others."

He left the room and I stood in the doorway, biting my lip and watching him make his way down the passage. I turned and faced Dehan and we stared at each other for a long moment. It was a strange habit we had fallen into shortly after we met. It made other people uncomfortable, but it helped us to think. After a moment, she blinked and ran her fingers through her hair.

"Well, at least we know it wasn't Gordon or Pamela."

I frowned at her. "I wasn't kidding, Dehan. I know who did it. I should have seen this coming. Our killer is crazy and almost unbelievably daring. This . . ." I gestured at Gordon. "This, while people were just feet away in the corridor—it is reckless to the point of insanity. But there is also a coldness to it, a clarity of thinking that, if we are not very careful, will lead to the killer being acquitted. There will be no evidence to convict them. The problem is not who did it, or even how. Both of those are obvious. The question, Dehan, is how do we prove it?"

NINETEEN

SALLY WAS LYING DOWN WITH HER FOREARM ACROSS her eyes. Bee was sitting next to her, holding her knees up to her chest and staring vacantly at the air six inches in front of her nose. The major was in an armchair by the window, watching her quietly. Cameron was on the floor, echoing Bee's position, but with his arms laid across the tops of his knees and his forehead on his arms. In the corner, Armstrong lay curled in the fetal position, snoring softly. Outside the door, the red-haired maid sat asleep in a chair. Beside her, Brown sat in another, drawn and anxious, watching me and Dehan.

I leaned on the doorjamb, and after a moment Bee turned to look at me. "Do you really, seriously think that one of us did these terrible things, Mr. Stone? Don't you think that your theories have perhaps gone a little astray?"

Dehan came up beside me, leaned on me, and rested her head on my shoulder. After a moment, I nodded. "No to the first and yes to the second, Bee." I jerked my head at the window, where the sky was already turning pale. "The storm has pretty much blown over. Phones should be working again soon." I shrugged. "I thought I'd cracked it, but the fact is I hadn't. And you know what? My wife and I came here on honeymoon, not to conduct a pro bono investigation, and frankly, if I'm honest, we are both pretty tired of getting insulted, sneered at, and put down for no other reason than we are Americans and work for the NYPD. We tried to help, I'm sorry it didn't work out."

Cameron looked up at us. His eyes were resentful. "I told you from the start you were on the wrong track. It was Gordon. It had to be."

Dehan snapped, "How! How'd he do it?"

"I don't know, but . . ."

"When you do know, talk. In the meantime, why don't you keep your mouth shut!"

Bee sighed. "It would be a relief if you did, Doctor."

I said, "The fact is, everybody has an alibi for the time of Gordon Sr.'s death. So either it was somebody who was not a member of the party in the house, or it was suicide, as the doctor says. Either way, Dehan and I are washing our hands of the case. We will call the cops as soon as we have a signal, we will preserve the crime scenes, and we will pass on our findings, such as they are, when they get here. But other than that, we are done. I do recommend, though, that you all lock your doors when you go to bed. There is at least a chance that there is a killer at large on the island, if not in this house."

With that I turned and made my way downstairs, with Dehan by my side. Above, I could hear them all leaving the room. We crossed the hall, and I undid the padlock on the study door, stepped inside, and pushed the door to behind us. I checked my cell. "Still no signal."

She picked up the landline and shook her head. She waited a moment, then started to dial and after a moment started to speak in a loud voice, as though she was talking to the cops. I moved quickly to the bay window, opened the left panel, and climbed out. Then I sprinted around the side of the house, past the steps down to the kitchen and in among the rosemary bushes in the orchard garden. There I lay flat, watching the side of the house, and waited.

I didn't have to wait long, maybe only fifteen minutes, but it felt a lot longer in the sodden, muddy soil after the storm. There was a dull grayness in the east, showing through wet, broken clouds that looked like they had been shredded by the wind and abandoned, scattered across the heavens. The light through the leaded windows in the tower looked warm and inviting in the paling predawn. I checked my watch. It was almost three.

Then I heard the soft clunk of the front door. A shadow stepped out and moved swiftly down the steps and into the driveway, then seemed to disappear. For a moment I wondered if I had somehow got it wrong, but after a moment, the same figure moved quickly and silently past the kitchen steps and stopped in front of me. There was a soft rustle, then the clink of a key, then the shadow shifted, moved away, and approached the side of the house. I heard the rattle of a lock, the soft squeak of a hinge, and the pad of feet descending stone steps into an enclosed space. I smiled, got to my feet, and crossed to the open door of the toolshed.

Just inside the door, I could make out the pale glow of worn stone steps. I sat on the top step and pressed the flashlight mode on my phone. He spun in the glare and stared at me, squinting and shielding his eyes, but all he could see was the glare of light. He moved fast, seizing a pitchfork that was standing in the corner, and took two steps toward me before he heard the click of the Smith & Wesson as Dehan sat down beside me and cocked the hammer.

I said, "Robert Armstrong, I am making a citizen's arrest. I arrest you for the murder of Charles Gordon Sr., and the attempted murder of Pamela Gordon. You do not have to say anything, and in fact we'd thank you if you didn't. But if you don't put that fork down in the next three seconds, I will give my pet rottweiler here permission to blow your balls off. Put it down, Armstrong. It's over."

He dropped the fork and raised his hands. I stood and made my way down the steps into the semisubterranean room. It was like the broom cupboard inside the house, and in fact it ran on from it, but about four and a half or five feet lower in the ground. Behind me, Dehan flipped a switch and a bare bulb overhead came on, filling the long, narrow room with a sickly light. I switched my phone from flashlight to video and handed it to Dehan.

At the far end of the shed there was a collection of spades, shovels, and other tools for gardening. On the floor, there were plastic and terra-cotta flowerpots, bags of compost, coils of hosepipe, and a hundred other things a gardener might use. Running the length of the left wall, from the steps to the end, up to a height of about four feet, there were shelves, with everything from balls of string to spray bottles and tins of paint. Above that, the wall was bare brick, aside from a small, freestanding bookcase affixed to the wall just above the shelves. It was about three feet square, almost reaching the ceiling. It was made of old, dark wood and held books on gardening.

I jerked my head at it. "Is that it?"

"Fuck yous."

I reached over, unhooked the bookcase, and set it on the floor. Behind it, there was just the bare, redbrick wall. I studied it a minute, then began to see where the old cement had been chipped away and new cement applied in its place. It had not yet had time to dry completely. I looked along the shelf and saw the plastic tub where he had mixed it and the spatula he'd used to apply it. I bagged the spatula and pulled my Swiss Army knife from my pocket, then began to remove the wet cement from the bricks. It was a segment of four in total: one above, one below, and two sandwiched between them. They were at head height, and as I eased them out of the wall, they revealed a hole, roughly the shape of a plus sign, in which the vertical line is short and fat. The hole, as I had expected, was in the back of the fireplace, directly behind the grate, and would, when the fire was burning, be concealed by the flames and the burning logs.

I turned to Dehan. "So you see, my dear Watson, the killer was never in the room. He took his shot from the toolshed."

Armstrong was staring at me and at Dehan by turns. "How did you know? How could you possibly have known?" He jerked his head at Dehan. "You were on the phone when I came down. I heard you. How could you have known I was here?"

I smiled. "I didn't, but I knew you would come here. I figured I'd worried you enough by saying I knew how it was done that you would come down and try to conceal the fresh cement and the tools you'd used to remove the bricks and cement them back in place. All I had to do was wait for you to show while you thought we were calling the cops." I reached behind him and propelled him toward Dehan on the steps. "Let's go, the game is over. You're done killing people."

We took him past the kitchen steps and back into the house. In the drawing room we put him on the sofa, tied his wrists and his ankles with his shoelaces, and sat with him until four, trying the phone at regular intervals. Finally, as the molten edge of the sun began to creep over the rim of a wet and sparkling world, the landline began to buzz, telling us we could phone. Then I took the handset out onto the front steps and made two calls. One of them was to the local Scottish PD to request urgent assistance and to discuss a few details with them.

After that, I went back inside to wake up and assemble the household.

The first to appear were Brown and the two maids. They looked in astonishment at Armstrong and then hurried away to the kitchen to start making breakfast. I stopped Brown at the door.

"Perhaps," I said, "you could give priority to a large pot of strong coffee and a couple of bacon sandwiches?"

"Oh, yes, naturally, sir."

He nodded and left. I opened the door that connected the drawing room to the dining room and before long, the major appeared. He was neat and spotlessly groomed as ever, but he had bags under his eyes from lack of sleep and his face was drawn and pale. He poked his head around the door, holding a cup and saucer in his hand, and frowned at us.

"Up early . . ."

I smiled. "We haven't been to bed yet. We went on a little hunting expedition last night. The cops are on their way, with the ME."

"Hunting, ay?" He kept narrowing his eyes at Armstrong. He took a few steps into the room and then his eyes widened. "Good Lord, are you bound, man?"

Dehan said, "With his own bootlaces."

Bee came in next, looking about as lively as the major. She peered distastefully at Armstrong and muttered, "Oh dear . . ." Then she sat and sipped silently at her cup of tea.

Cameron came down a little later, looking disheveled and as though he had slept in his clothes. He was supporting Pamela who had, it seemed, been given a powerful tranquilizer but nothing more serious than that. Sometimes, I told myself, the victim just gets lucky. And then wondered if she would agree.

Finally, Sally came in, looking about as rough as her husband. They were all assembled, sitting around the room much as they had on that first night, only with two notable exceptions. When we had arrived, the major had told us about the murder of Grandfather Gordon. Now the father and the son were dead too.

They all sat and silently watched me and Dehan, and occasionally they glanced at Armstrong. Nobody asked, so when I had finished my coffee I got to my feet and went and stood over by the fireplace.

"It's hard to know exactly where to begin. The story goes back more than forty years." I smiled. "So we may as well start at the end. It's as good a place as any. Let's begin last night, when you, Major, and Charles Jr. had finished showing us the study. You went to join Bee, and Dehan and I went upstairs. We were surprised, when we reached the landing, to see Mr. Armstrong come in from the storm. We were surprised because when he had brought us back from the village a little earlier in his taxi, he had dropped us at the gate, claiming he would not set foot in this house on account of the fact that Charles Gordon Sr. was, in his words, a thieving bastard." I paused. "Yet it turned out that Mr. Armstrong not only frequently set foot in the house, but had done so for many years as the gardener. So, logically, his decision not to set foot here was a recent one, even though Mr. Gordon's alleged thieving had occurred almost forty years ago."

I paused. They were all frowning.

I said, "It's a bit of a mess, but let me try and simplify. According to Mr. Armstrong, forty years ago Gordon Sr. stole his inheritance, but Mr. Armstrong did not complain about it for almost forty years. Then, quite suddenly, very recently, he decided he was so mad about it he would not set foot in the house. And no sooner had he decided that, than he went and set foot in the house, according to him, because he had business to settle with one of the Gordons."

There was a lot of ass-shifting and a lot of glancing sidelong at Armstrong, who was staring sullenly at the floor.

"Dehan and I assumed that he had come to see Charles Jr. in his study. Charles had stayed there to do some work, as he apparently often did, and as Armstrong must have known, having spent many years working here. But in fact, Armstrong had a very different purpose. He knew, as probably the whole island does by now, that Gordon Sr. kept his Smith and Wesson service revolver in his bedroom. How often had you talked about it in your day, Pam? And you, Sally?"

Sally's voice was a dry rasp. "More than once," she said.

I nodded. "And the bush telegraph took care of the rest. It had been common knowledge for a long time. And, for reasons I'll come to in a minute, Armstrong had special reasons for knowing.

"The point is, when we thought he was going in to see Charles in the study, what he actually did, when we had gone into our own room, was to go up to the master bedroom and get the revolver. He then went down to the toolshed, where he had carefully removed four of the bricks from precisely the right place behind the logs, and he shot young Charles Gordon Jr. in the head.

"He took his time replacing the bricks, and the cement, and then came back into the house. He then put on the show for us of shouting and kicking down the door, but of course, before anybody could get to him, he had entered the room, squeezed the gun into Charles' hand, and dropped it by his side. The perfect closed-room murder, exactly like his grandfather's forty years earlier. And like his grandfather, the only possible explanation would be suicide.

"Later, when we had finished taking your statements and I announced that I knew who had committed the homicide and how, it was Mr. Armstrong who deliberately started a row, by accusing you, Sally, of having an affair with both Gordon Sr. and Jr. While the room was in commotion, he took a syringe and what he mistakenly thought was a lethal dose of sedative from Dr. Cameron's bag. It was daring in the extreme, but Mr. Armstrong is nothing if not daring, *and* extreme.

"When everybody went up, after Brown had shown him to his room, he slipped back to Pamela's room and injected her in the sole of her foot, where the mark would be almost invisible. He assumed that the sedative, on top of the tablets she had already taken, would constitute a lethal dose. Fortunately, what he injected her with was Midazolam, a powerful tranquilizer that is nonlethal. He then flushed the tablets Cameron had left her down the can to make it look as though she had overdosed, and he slipped out of the room, taking the syringe with him.

"From there, he went straight to the master bedroom and tapped on the door. When Gordon opened up, he threatened him with the syringe to his neck. I'm guessing you told him it had bleach in it, or some ghastly concoction; or maybe you threatened him with an air bubble. Either way, you scared him enough to make him climb on his own gun-box and put a noose around his neck rather than try and fight you. Maybe, like most bullies, at heart he was a coward.

"I'm guessing you made him tie his own noose, you made him stand on the box, and then you kicked the box out from under him." I shook my head. "It was outrageously daring, and it almost worked. But you made a few mistakes, and one of them was not to leave the box on the floor where it fell."

He stared sullenly at me but made no response.

I turned back to the watching faces. "He flushed the needle down the toilet, rushed around to Pam's room, where Bee was raising the alarm, and dropped the syringe into the bag." I turned back to Armstrong. "I don't know if you wiped your prints off. I do know you didn't use surgical gloves for any of this. The chances are good they'll get your prints on the syringe, and on Pam's ankle, and two gets you twenty there are latents on the revolver."

"But . . ." It was the major, staring at me with narrowed eyes. "What I don't understand is, *why?*"

But I had already started to hear the throb of approaching choppers outside.

TWENTY

IT WAS AN AIR AMBULANCE AND A POLICE HELICOPTER.
Dehan and I stepped out to watch them land near the driveway in
a vast cloud of mist kicked up from the sodden grass by the down-
draft from the rotors.

As the whine of the turbines died and the throb slowly stilled,
men and women began to spill from the two choppers. From the
air ambulance, paramedics in cumbersome, high-visibility gear
came running with stretchers, followed by a man in a tweed jacket
carrying a black leather satchel. I hailed them and as they
approached, I pointed back at the house. "You have a possible
overdose on sleeping tablets in the drawing room on the left."

They began to move.

I said, "Listen to me. She was an intended murder victim and
was injected with an unknown amount of Midazolam. She had
already taken two sleeping tablets before that. Ask for Dr.
Cameron. He's in there with her."

They took it in and moved toward the house at a steady trot. I
turned to the guy in the tweed jacket. "Are you the ME?"

"I am. Who are you?"

"A guest at the hotel and a detective with the NYPD." I
handed him the keys to the study. "You have one body in the

study on the right as you go in. Another upstairs in the master bedroom. Downstairs is a .38 gunshot wound to the head. Upstairs, he was hanged."

I might as well have told him it had rained. He walked away saying, "Och, you've had a busy night, then."

Two cops in uniform and three men in suits were approaching us from the other helicopter. One of the plainclothes looked worried; the other was smiling. He was in his fifties, well-groomed and well-built, with intelligent, humorous eyes.

He spoke from fifteen feet away, holding out his hand and laughing. "John Stone, as I live and breathe! Am I in the Orkneys or in some kind of Bond movie?"

"Henry." I gripped his hand and shook it with pleasure. "When you find out, will you tell me? This is Carmen, my wife and my partner in the PD."

They shook. "I'm impressed with the NYPD's latest line in detective uniforms, I must say. Very fetching. This is Inspector Harris, from Thurso, and Mr. Mackenzie of Mackenzie and Hennessy, solicitors, also of Thurso."

Harris took my hand and shook it vigorously. "Uz et troo?" he asked.

"Which bit?" I asked back.

"That Gordon an' his bairn are deed?"

I nodded. "Yes, the ME is looking at the bodies as we speak. It was pure luck that Mrs. Gordon was not killed too."

Mackenzie reached over and shook my hand too. "And they were murdered, you say? In what order? And by whom?"

I smiled and nodded at him. "I thought you'd be asking those questions. We'll come to all that in due course. Mr. Mackenzie, I want to ask you a favor. If you should happen to see anybody you recognize from your office, please don't react. Just ignore them, would you? It's important."

Henry was watching me closely with narrowed eyes. "But you say that you have not only solved these murders, but also the original murder of forty years ago."

I nodded. "Yes. I am just waiting for one last person to arrive . . . Ah, I think this is her now."

A Ford Mondeo was speeding down the drive toward the house. I said, "Shall we go in?"

Henry turned to Dehan. "What on Earth made you marry him? How do you stand him? He's so smug."

She raised an eyebrow at him. "You think *that's* a problem? This is supposed to be our honeymoon!"

Henry laughed and we made our way back to the stone steps that led up to the door, just as the Mondeo pulled up and a young woman in her late twenties clambered out. She saw us, looked at Mackenzie, and stopped dead. Mackenzie frowned and looked away, mumbling something. She suddenly blurted out, "I'm looking fer Bobby Armstrong. I was told he was here! Is he okay?"

I smiled. "Yes, he's as well as can be expected. It was me who called you. Please, come this way."

And we all filed into the drawing room again.

Armstrong went pale and half stood as Lizzie came in. "Lizzie! What on Earth . . . !" Then he saw Mackenzie. Lizzie rushed to Armstrong and flung her arms around his neck, realizing too late that he was bound hand and foot. He fell back and she staggered, then turned to stare at me.

I turned to Harris. "Perhaps, Inspector, you could have one of your men replace those bootlaces with handcuffs. I left mine in New York."

"It's a trap!" she hissed. "You let yourself get bloody trapped!"

Mackenzie coughed. "I think, Mr. Stone, that it is probably high time you explained to us exactly what is going on, and why my secretary is here, with Mr. Armstrong, instead of at her desk, where she belongs!"

Harris nodded at one of his constables, who crossed the room and started untying Armstrong's bonds. While he did it, I said, "I couldn't agree more, Mr. Mackenzie. It is, as you say, high time. You'd better make yourselves comfortable, this is going to take some explaining."

The constables were dispatched to help the medical examiner in the study, and Mackenzie and Henry took their seats. Dehan sat in a large armchair beside the cold fireplace, and I sat on the arm of her chair. I looked at Henry and smiled.

"Most of this is simple, logical deduction, some of it is surmise, most or all of it I hope you will be able to prove with what little forensic evidence we have been able to secure.

"This all starts about forty years ago, when Old Man Gordon, a wealthy Bostonian who had become obsessed with his Scottish roots and his family history, moved back to the north of Scotland and bought an island, and a castle, which according to his research had belonged to his ancestors. With time, his obsession grew, and I guess he came to see himself as an ancient, Celtic Laird ruling over his island kingdom, owning his subjects and striving to keep the bloodlines pure. And that last point is important because, as I found out from the family library, Old Man Gordon's late wife had not been a Gordon. She was not from any of the great clans. In fact, she was not even Scottish. Her family, to the old man's enduring horror, was of English descent. Her name was Sarah Culpepper. I can only assume that his obsession with all things Scottish began to grow *after* he had married and sired his son, the late Charles Gordon Sr."

Mackenzie shifted in his chair and gave a small cough. "Are we to understand, then, Mr. Stone, that Charles Gordon Sr. was in fact only *half* Scottish?"

I nodded. "And half English."

Armstrong curled his lip. "Well, no'ne's perfect, eh, Ian?"

Dehan raised an eyebrow at him. "Some less than others, pal."

"The point is," I went on, "that the old man became increasingly troubled by what he saw as his son's imperfection. It was like an itch he couldn't scratch. Meantime, while Charles was at university in Boston, two things happened. The old man, who liked, as it were, to move among his subjects, met a very young and very attractive Pamela May at the local inn. Presumably he had nothing particularly *against* commoners who did not belong to the great clans. Especially when they looked like Pam. He didn't mind sleeping with them, he just didn't want to marry them and breed with them. She was attractive and had an engaging personality, and he had money and power. They both had something the other wanted, and they started an affair.

"The other thing that happened was that he met Mrs. Armstrong and young Bobby, who at that time would have been just a young teenager. It is somewhat ironic that these two encounters, which were life-defining for him, would ultimately lead to his death and the destruction of what he saw as his dynasty.

"Pam saw Old Man Gordon as a potential way out of an island and a way of life that to her was a prison. But Mrs. Armstrong was, to Old Man Gordon, the answer to his prayers. Here was a woman of pure Scottish stock, descended from Gordons and with a son who carried the blood of two of the great clans. Pam didn't stand a chance, and Charles, away at university in Boston, was on a very slippery slope.

"When he graduated and came home, it was to discover that he had all but been disinherited in favor of young Robert Armstrong. His father planned to marry Mrs. Armstrong, and when he did, he planned to amend his will." I gestured at Mackenzie. "Correct me if I am wrong, but as I understand it, the old man had decided, through some strange sense of propriety, to go through two stages . . ."

Mackenzie nodded. "That is correct. He felt that until he was married, his estate should go to his own son, so what he had us do was to draw up a will in which his son was the beneficiary of the estate *until he died*, and *after* his death it would pass to Mr. Armstrong. Mr. Gordon would effectively hold the estate on trust for Mr. Armstrong. This was never intended to be a long-term solution. He was merely protecting himself until such time as they were married, when he intended to leave his entire estate to his new wife and her son, bar a small endowment to his son."

I nodded. "Thank you, that was how I understood it. It must

have been quite a shock to Charles when he got home to discover that he had gone from being the heir to a fortune to being just like the rest of us. He sought, and found, solace in Pamela May. I am pretty sure he never told her, or anybody else, the exact nature of what his father had done, or Pamela would have dropped him like a hot brick. And at that time, he was pretty sweet on Pamela. Equally, Pamela did not tell him that she had been engaged in an affair with his father.

"Charles decided to marry Pamela. He was in love with her and, after all, had nothing to lose. He had already lost everything. But then, out of resentment and anger, or perhaps because he had inherited some of his father's craziness, he hatched a plan. We will never know for sure, but I am guessing that he had access to a copy of the will and he studied it in detail. Again, correct me if I am wrong, Mr. Mackenzie, but the will said that if Old Man Gordon were to die *before* his marriage to Mrs. Armstrong, the estate would go to Charles until his death, when it would pass to the Armstrongs."

"That is correct."

"So the answer was simple. He had to kill his father and make it look like a suicide. The old man had a reputation for being eccentric, so nobody would be that surprised if he did something crazy like shoot himself. If, in addition, he staged it so that it seemed his father had had some kind of emotional crisis and seen the error of his ways, the suicide scenario would be even more credible.

"What he did next was very ingenious. It had struck me from the start that there was a curious feature to this case: though the old man was supposed to have shot himself in the study with a Smith and Wesson .38, nobody in the house had heard the shot. A .38 revolver is not quiet! And this happened again when Charles Jr. was killed. The reason was simple.

"There is, where the tower ends and the ballroom begins, a gap between the two structures of about seven feet. I don't know what its purpose was originally, but now it houses a broom cupboard on the inside, and on the outside a toolshed. The interesting thing is that the toolshed is sunk about four or five feet below ground level . . ."

Pam spoke for the first time in a voice that was weary and drained of life. She shook her head. "There is no great mystery there, Mr. Stone. Many old houses have something similar. You pick a harvest of potatoes or apples, and you store them below ground level in the dark; they will last the winter that way. There are several such nooks around the house."

"Well, this one was unique in that the southern wall was in fact the north wall of the study, and one very particular spot gave onto the fireplace." I smiled at Henry and saw him close his eyes and sigh. "We are least likely to see what is right before our eyes. Just about the center of the fireplace, inside the toolshed, was at a height of about five and a half feet. Charles took his time, identified the exact spot, and gradually carved away the cement from four of the bricks at just about head height. He left them attached to each other, so that he could slide them out as a single unit. The constant use of the fire meant that any irregularity in the bricks was quickly blackened and covered in soot.

"On the day of the murder, he made a point of telling everyone in the household that he planned to talk to his father about his intention to marry Pam. His father was in the habit of locking himself in the study when he worked. So, when his father was engrossed in his research on the history of his family, Charles went to the toolshed, removed the bricks, and shot him in the head. With remarkable coolness, he then put back the bricks, went about the house giving everybody the good news that his father had agreed to the marriage, and went dashing off to tell Pamela.

"He then returned, with the revolver in his pocket, broke down the door, squeezed the revolver into his father's hand, and then dropped it on the floor to make it seem he had shot himself. By this time, a good hour or more since the murder, the fire and smoke had completely erased any sign of the bricks having been removed.

"When everybody arrived at the scene just moments later, it was to find a suicide. My good friend Henry spotted the inconsistencies, the lack of GSR on the old man's hand, the trajectory of the bullet, the lack of scorching around the entry wound. But following the Holmesian dictum, eliminate the impossible . . ." I shrugged. "It seemed that the impossible was that it was murder; therefore, however unlikely, by some fluke the GSR had been blown away from the hand and the gun's recoil had altered the trajectory of the slug, yadda yadda—in short, it was suicide.

"But in fact, the impossible was that it was suicide. And if it was impossible for the murderer to have been in the room, then the murderer had to be *outside* the room. That meant he shot through a hole which he later covered up. Once you accepted that, it was not hard to see where that hole had been, because, as you correctly deduced, Henry, the shot came from the fireplace."

Henry did a lot of slow nodding, then smiled at Dehan. "I'll ask you again, Carmen, how do you tolerate him?"

She offered him a lopsided smile. "He takes me on these amazing holidays."

Inspector Harris was scratching his head. "But, hold on there a munit, are you sayin' that Mr. Gordon Sr. mardard his own father *and* his own son? An', if so, why is Mr. Armstrong in cuffs?"

I shook my head. "No. Mr. Gordon killed his father and inherited the estate on the terms of the will, as you have described them, holding it on trust for the Armstrongs. But Mr. Armstrong did not know the terms of the will, and Mr. Gordon was not about to tell him.

"Now, Mr. Armstrong was the gardener. He was familiar with the toolshed and he had no doubt about how his employer had pulled off the murder. The thing was, he would never be able to prove it, and so he had no choice but to accept almost forty years of humiliation—and Charles Sr. did enjoy inflicting a bit of humiliation on those around him—working as a gardener in the house that he knew the old man had intended to be his.

"Then, almost forty years later, he hooks up with a young lady who works as a secretary at the very law firm where Gordon's will is safely stashed away. Now, if Old Man Gordon was obsessed with his heritage, so was Robert Armstrong, but in a very different way. It is not long before he tells his girlfriend, Lizzie, all about it, and she says to him, 'Why don't I sneak a look at the will and see if there is anything in it that we can use to claim your inheritance?' But what she finds is a bombshell. What she finds is that as soon as Charles Sr. dies, the estate passes to the Armstrongs."

I looked at Armstrong and Lizzie. "They found exactly what Gordon had found all those years before, that the only thing standing between them and a fortune was another man's life. And Armstrong already knew how Charles Sr. had done it. All he had to do was repeat the exercise.

"But, there was a hitch, that safety clause that the old man had put into the will—if Old Man Gordon were to die before marrying Mrs. Armstrong, and upon his death his son were still alive and in residence at the castle, then the estate would go to his son." I paused and nodded, looking at Pam. "But, of course, it was rumored all over the island—and nobody knew for sure whether it was true or not—that *both* Charles Sr. and Charles Jr. were Old Man Gordon's sons. It was even odds that they were not father and son, but half brothers. So they *both* had to be eliminated. Did you ever have his paternity checked, Pam?"

She shook her head. "They were both as bad as each other. Charles was my son, not theirs. He was good and kind and gentle, nothing like either of them." She stared at me a moment. "If he did it, why did he always maintain it was murder?"

I shrugged. "What better cover?"

She sighed, then looked at Mackenzie. "So what happens to me now? Do I lose everything?"

He shook his head. "Not at all. Old Man Gordon was very

concerned not to be taken advantage of. He was as canny as a Scotsman, even if he was an American. He had it written into the will that if he or his son were murdered, the trust would fail and the entire estate would go to his immediate next of kin. That would be you, Mrs. Gordon."

Armstrong leaned forward on the sofa, his face crimson and the veins in his head swollen and pulsing. He screamed, "*Ut's mine, you filthy, whooring bitch! Ut's mine! D'ya hear! Mine!*"

She didn't flinch. She watched him coolly and when he'd finished, she softly shook her head. "No, Bobby Armstrong. It's *mine.*"

EPILOGUE

"IT'S THE GULF STREAM," I SAID. "IT COMES ALL THE way from Mexico, bringing warm currents and warm air."

The full moon was sitting about four inches above the horizon, laying a deceptive path of liquid light across an inky ocean to a soft, sandy shore, where small waves spilled onto the beach and then sighed as they withdrew back into the deep.

Dehan pulled the bottle of white wine from the ice bucket we had stuck in the sand between us and refilled my glass and hers.

"I don't care," she said. "England is supposed to be foggy and rainy, with cute red phone boxes and big green hedgerows. It is not supposed to have palm trees and white sandy beaches."

I shrugged. "This is Cornwall. Cornwall is different."

She sipped. "This is a weird island."

"It's a weird archipelago."

"Good weird, but weird." She was quiet for a moment, then said, "So Pam is paying for this?"

"She insisted. She wanted to honor her husband's commitment."

"So you thought you'd go for a two-week tour of five-star hotels in a self-drive classic car at two thousand bucks a week."

"It's an Aston Martin DB6, like the one James Bond drove. I

thought it was fair. I ruined my tuxedo to save her castle, it was the least she could do."

She rested her head on my shoulder and we both sipped. "You're about as weird as this archipelago, you know that."

"It's why you like me. You're as weird as I am."

"You never did tell me what your connection is with this place."

"Nope, but I will."

She sighed. "So where to tomorrow?"

"I thought we'd stay at the Old Parsonage in Oxford and then move on to the Ritz in London. There we can go to the opera at Covent Garden before flying back on Friday."

She was quiet for a while, then said, "Back to the Bronx and the Forty-Third Precinct."

I nodded. A cool breeze blew in off the sea and touched our skin. I kissed the top of her head.

"It's the same moon, you know, here and there."

Don't miss THE BUTCHER OF WHITEC.
sequel in the Dead Cold Mystery

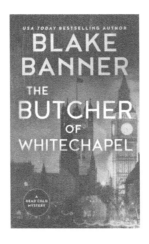

Scan the QR code below to purchase THE BUTCHER OF WHITECHAPEL.

Or go to: righthouse.com/the-butcher-of-whitechapel

NOTE: flip to the very end to read an exclusive sneak peak...

DON'T MISS ANYTHING!

If you want to stay up to date on all new releases in this series, with this author, or with any of our new deals, you can do so by joining our newsletters below.

In addition, you will immediately gain access to our entire *Right House VIP Library*, which includes many riveting Mystery and Thriller novels for your enjoyment!

righthouse.com/email

(Easy to unsubscribe. No spam. Ever.)

ALSO BY BLAKE BANNER

Up to date books can be found at:
www.righthouse.com/blake-banner

ROGUE THRILLERS
Gates of Hell (Book 1)
Hell's Fury (Book 2)

ALEX MASON THRILLERS
Odin (Book 1)
Ice Cold Spy (Book 2)
Mason's Law (Book 3)
Assets and Liabilities (Book 4)
Russian Roulette (Book 5)
Executive Order (Book 6)
Dead Man Talking (Book 7)
All The King's Men (Book 8)
Flashpoint (Book 9)
Brotherhood of the Goat (Book 10)
Dead Hot (Book 11)
Blood on Megiddo (Book 12)
Son of Hell (Book 13)

HARRY BAUER THRILLER SERIES
Dead of Night (Book 1)
Dying Breath (Book 2)
The Einstaat Brief (Book 3)
Quantum Kill (Book 4)
Immortal Hate (Book 5)
The Silent Blade (Book 6)
LA: Wild Justice (Book 7)

Breath of Hell (Book 8)
Invisible Evil (Book 9)
The Shadow of Ukupacha (Book 10)
Sweet Razor Cut (Book 11)
Blood of the Innocent (Book 12)
Blood on Balthazar (Book 13)
Simple Kill (Book 14)
Riding The Devil (Book 15)
The Unavenged (Book 16)
The Devil's Vengeance (Book 17)
Bloody Retribution (Book 18)
Rogue Kill (Book 19)
Blood for Blood (Book 20)

DEAD COLD MYSTERY SERIES
An Ace and a Pair (Book 1)
Two Bare Arms (Book 2)
Garden of the Damned (Book 3)
Let Us Prey (Book 4)
The Sins of the Father (Book 5)
Strange and Sinister Path (Book 6)
The Heart to Kill (Book 7)
Unnatural Murder (Book 8)
Fire from Heaven (Book 9)
To Kill Upon A Kiss (Book 10)
Murder Most Scottish (Book 11)
The Butcher of Whitechapel (Book 12)
Little Dead Riding Hood (Book 13)
Trick or Treat (Book 14)
Blood Into Wine (Book 15)
Jack In The Box (Book 16)
The Fall Moon (Book 17)
Blood In Babylon (Book 18)
Death In Dexter (Book 19)
Mustang Sally (Book 20)

A Christmas Killing (Book 21)
Mommy's Little Killer (Book 22)
Bleed Out (Book 23)
Dead and Buried (Book 24)
In Hot Blood (Book 25)
Fallen Angels (Book 26)
Knife Edge (Book 27)
Along Came A Spider (Book 28)
Cold Blood (Book 29)
Curtain Call (Book 30)

THE OMEGA SERIES
Dawn of the Hunter (Book 1)
Double Edged Blade (Book 2)
The Storm (Book 3)
The Hand of War (Book 4)
A Harvest of Blood (Book 5)
To Rule in Hell (Book 6)
Kill: One (Book 7)
Powder Burn (Book 8)
Kill: Two (Book 9)
Unleashed (Book 10)
The Omicron Kill (Book 11)
9mm Justice (Book 12)
Kill: Four (Book 13)
Death In Freedom (Book 14)
Endgame (Book 15)

ABOUT US

Right House is an independent publisher created by authors for readers. We specialize in Action, Thriller, Mystery, and Crime novels.

If you enjoyed this novel, then there is a good chance you will like what else we have to offer! Please stay up to date by using any of the links below.

Join our mailing lists to stay up to date --> righthouse.com/email
Visit our website --> righthouse.com
Contact us --> contact@righthouse.com

 facebook.com/righthousebooks

 x.com/righthousebooks

 instagram.com/righthousebooks

EXCLUSIVE SNEAK PEAK OF...

THE BUTCHER OF WHITECHAPEL

CHAPTER 1

Our American Airlines flight was due to depart from London Heathrow at five in the afternoon. We had decided to be there two hours earlier so that we could have time for a martini in the bar before boarding. That meant we had booked our taxi to the airport for two. So at one forty-five, we were in the lobby of our hotel on Piccadilly, settling our bill, while our luggage was taken out to await the cab, when my phone rang. The screen told me it was Inspector John Newman, the chief at our precinct in the Bronx.

I thumbed green and he spoke before I did.

"John, it's John. I hope you've had a great honeymoon."

"Thanks, we have. Not what we expected, but interesting[1]. We're just . . ."

"I imagine you're just about heading for the airport, are you . . . ?"

"Yup. That's what we're doing. Planning to have a . . ."

"Here's the thing, John. How would you feel about staying on a few days?"

I blinked at Dehan, who was watching me without expres-

---

1. See *Murder Most Scottish.*

then I held up a hand to the concierge and said into the phone, "Um . . ."

"I realize it's short notice . . ."

"I just settled the bill, sir."

"I think you'll find the reservation has been extended, as a courtesy . . ."

I stared a moment at Dehan, then at the concierge, who was frowning at his screen. "Our reservation has been extended . . . ?" I said, not quite sure whom I was asking.

Dehan screwed up her face and mouthed, "What?" and the concierge looked at me with raised eyebrows and nodded.

"What's this about, sir?"

"Your friend, Detective Inspector Henry Green, he's asked Scotland Yard to request you as a special consultant."

"A *consultant*? On what, sir?"

"Well, I'd better let him explain that. I think you'll find he's sent a car for you. Keep me posted, John. Enjoy your extended, um, honeymoon . . ."

The line went dead. Dehan gave me a "what the hell" shrug and the concierge said, "Shall I have your luggage taken back up, sir? It seems you are in the honeymoon suite for another week . . ." He raised an eyebrow. "Courtesy of Scotland Yard!"

"Yes, please. It seems we are."

Dehan smiled and raised both her eyebrows dangerously high toward her hairline. "Do I get a say in this?"

"Apparently not. That was the inspector. Henry has a car on the way. He will explain more fully when we see him, but it seems we are consulting for Scotland Yard, my dear Watson."

"Super."

We didn't have to wait long. Ten minutes later, a guy in his midtwenties with short, fair hair and dark glasses came in, scanning the foyer as he walked. His eyes fell on us where we were sitting and he approached, removing his glasses and smiling without his eyes. "Mr. and Mrs. Stone?"

We stood. "Are you the man from Scotland Yard?"

We shook. "Detective Inspector Green asked me to come over and fetch you. My car is outside." He glanced around. "Nice. We don't usually put people up at the Ritz."

Dehan grunted. "Yeah, it's a long story. Any idea what this is about?"

"I think DI Green had better explain that, ma'am."

New York, like all American cities, was designed on purpose by men imbued with the ideals of the Age of Reason and empirical logic, who thought, for better or worse, that it made sense to lay out the roads in a grid.

London was not designed on purpose. It grew organically over more than two thousand years, and the roads, lanes, and streets—or at least most of them—follow paths laid down first by nomadic hunter-gatherers, then by cattle herders and farmers bringing their goods to market, and after that by the increasing ebb and flow of people: drawn to the docks that send out ships and adventurers to the world's greatest empire, and receive its bounty in return; and to the narrow, cobbled streets and dark taverns of Westminster, where men plotted on how to relieve the Spanish of their ill-gotten gold, and how to squash upstart French emperors. The streets of London reflect all of that to this day.

We wound and wove and wended our way among an extraordinary mismatch of buildings that comprised the ultra-modern in glass and steel and the ultra-ancient in crooked timber and plaster and all kinds of stuff in between, including '30s functional and post-Blitz hideous. We eventually came out onto Whitechapel Road, which is long and dreary and ugly and seems to go on forever, until finally, we turned right at a large intersection into New Road. From there we made a left into Newark Street and right into Halcrow Street and stopped outside a dark blue door with a brass knob and a brass number 1 on it.

The street was just seven houses long, and most of it was taken up with the police presence: there were a couple of uniforms outside the door in reflective yellow jackets, white police tape had been deployed across the length of the house, and there were two patrol cars, an unmarked VW, a crime scene van, and an ambulance, all blocking the road.

The driver smiled at us in the mirror, without making it look like a smile, and said, "DI Green will be inside. Have a good one."

We thanked him and climbed out. A uniformed sergeant approached with curious eyes that didn't quite conceal a mixture of hostility and amusement. "Help you, sir, madam?"

I didn't hold it against him. I could imagine how the boys and girls at the 43rd would feel if a guy from Scotland Yard was shipped in to "consult" for us on one of our cases. I smiled. "I don't know. We were boarding a plane and DI Green sent for us. I have no idea what this is about." I nodded at the door. "I believe he's inside."

He nodded. "Your names, sir, madam?"

"John Stone; this is my wife, Carmen Stone."

"Detectives Stone and Dehan," he said, "of the NYPD." It wasn't a question. He raised the tape for us to pass through.

I said, "We're supposed to be on holiday."

He grinned. "Not anymore, you're not. Right at the top. Heads up: it's not pretty."

We stepped through the door into a narrow hallway. The staircase ascended the left wall, and on the right, a passage led past two doors to a small kitchen at the back. We climbed the stairs to a small landing on the top floor. There, a woman in a white, plastic suit frowned at us and said, "Who are you?"

"John and Carmen Stone. DI Green sent for us."

"Oh," she said. "The Americans. He's in there. Try not to throw up, at least not in the room. It's a crime scene."

She squeezed past us and we stood back to let her by. Henry appeared at the door and stepped out to shake our hands. "John, Carmen, let me prepare you before you come in and have a look."

I nodded. "I'd appreciate that. What's going on, Henry? We were on our way to the airport."

He nodded and sighed. "I know, and I do apologize, but it will all become clear. John, I think you could be a real help to us on this." He glanced at Dehan. "No offense intended at all. But John has seen this before. He knows all about it. Go on in and have a look, John. Be prepared. It's not pretty."

The Brits have a genius for understatement. "Not pretty" was a young woman in her midtwenties, naked, laid out with her hands nailed to the wooden floor. Her legs were spread, suggesting she had been raped; there was the handle of a kitchen knife protruding from her left fifth intercostal where she had been stabbed through the heart; and her belly had been cut open from her solar plexus to her pubic bone, postmortem. There was also a piece of paper over her face with the end of a meat skewer sticking out of it.

The crime scene guys—the Brits call them SOCO—were dusting, examining, and photographing the room. I had a quick look around. There wasn't much to see at first glance. A white IKEA sofa, a chair to match, a coffee table, and a large, flat-screen TV. She was lying between the sofa and the TV. A door beside the sofa appeared to lead to a bedroom. I approached her head and hunkered down to look at the paper. The meat skewer was stuck through it, apparently into her eye. Somebody said, "Don't touch that, please."

I looked up at Henry. He was leaning on the doorjamb. Dehan was standing next to him, frowning at the body. I said, "The eyes were perforated?"

He nodded. "Both eyes."

"Postmortem?"

"Yup."

There was writing, something printed on the paper. I knew there would be, and I had a pretty good idea of what it would say, but I had to inch around to read it. Henry said, "It says what you think it says."

I read aloud, "And them good ole boys were drinking whisky and rye . . ."

I frowned, sighed, and stood. "Who is she? Is she an American?"

"Don't know. No idea who she is."

Dehan jerked her head toward the bedroom door. "What about her ID?"

I smiled at her. "The Brits don't carry ID."

She raised her eyebrows and smiled. "No shit?"

Henry gave a small laugh. "Not since the fifties. They keep trying to force us, but we love to be awkward. So far, we have no indication of who she is. We're tracking down the landlord . . ."

"Who called it in?"

"Neighbor downstairs, noticed her mail and her milk hadn't been collected."

She nodded, then, after a moment, shrugged. "So what's the deal?" She looked at me. "You're asking if she's American. She has part of the chorus to 'American Pie' stuck to her eye . . . why are we here? More to the point, why is *he* here?" She pointed at me.

Henry went to answer and I said, "Let's go downstairs."

Henry nodded. "Yeah, come on, we'll go to the Blind Beggar."

Dehan winced at him. "Really?"

He glanced at the girl nailed to the floor. "Yeah, sorry. The beer's better than the White Hart. Let's go."

We followed him down the narrow stairs and out into the late August afternoon. Overhead, heavy clouds were beginning to gather. He pointed to the unmarked VW and we climbed in, slammed the doors, and headed at speed down Sidney Street, back toward Whitechapel Road.

"You probably don't notice it," he said as he drove. "You haven't been here for what, fifteen years? The capital is changing. Everybody's leaving." I looked out the window. It seemed to me that London's eight million inhabitants were all out at the same time.

Dehan spoke from the back seat. "Are you sure about that?"

He laughed as he pulled up at the lights. "There are far fewer Europeans, and fewer refugees too. They're leaving in droves because of Brexit. And a lot of the Muslim population, they're worried that a far-right government, hostile to Muslims, might come to power. They are seeing France and Germany as more welcoming, and Spain."

The lights changed and we crossed over and parked beside an old redbrick Victorian pub with white stone embellishings, tall chimney stacks, and elaborate scrolls around the date 1894 right at the top.

The door rattled and clanged as we pushed inside. The public bar was almost empty. The walls were paneled in dark wood; there was an open fireplace, a long, highly polished bar with rows of big, wooden beer pumps, and a ginger cat sitting beside them, licking its paws.

We found a table and Henry went to the bar to get three pints of bitter. While he was gone, Dehan gave me a once-over and said, "If this were something normal, you would have told me about it by now. Why the big mystery?"

I took a deep breath and let it out slow through puffed cheeks. "It's what you've been asking me about since we got here, and what I have been avoiding talking about. Not . . ." I looked her in the eye. "Not because I don't want you to know about it, but because it is hard for me to talk about. But I guess now we are going to have to, whether I want to or not."

She frowned. "Okay . . ."

Right on cue, Henry returned with the pints and set them on the table. He glanced at us both as he did it and said, "I'm assuming, John, that you have already told Carmen about the Butcher of Whitechapel . . ."

I sucked my teeth and shook my head.

His jaw sagged a little. "Nothing at all . . . ?"

I shook my head again.

He looked at me with meaning. "*Nothing . . . ?*"

"Nothing, Henry. Nothing at all."

Dehan sighed. "Okay, guys, I think we have understood that I have been told *nothing at all* about the Butcher of Whitechapel. How about we set that right and somebody starts telling me?"

Henry picked up his glass, raised his eyebrows at me, and said, "Over to you, me old mucker."

I nodded.

"This was about fifteen, sixteen years ago, around the time I came over. There was a series of killings, all in Whitechapel. They were all young women in their early twenties, all blond, pretty, between five foot five and five-eight. There were four of them: Cindy Rogers, Amy Porter, Sally-Anne Sterling, and Kathleen Dodge. Kathleen Dodge was Canadian; the other three were American. They all worked at the Royal London Hospital, in Whitechapel."

I paused and took a pull from my pint. As I set the glass down, I went on. "Each one of them had been crucified on the floor in her own apartment. They had been stabbed in the heart with a large kitchen knife, they had each had their womb removed, without skill, and each one had had her eyes perforated postmortem. All the mutilations were postmortem. Each of the women showed signs of having been raped, but presumably he used a condom, because there was no trace of semen. And, each one had a note stabbed into her left eye with a meat skewer, with that same line from 'American Pie.'"

Henry was staring at me. I avoided his eye.

Dehan said, "I'm guessing you didn't catch him."

I nodded again. "The guys who were in charge of this end of the exchange program figured we have a lot more serial killers in the States than they have over here, which is true, and so they thought I should be on the task force. So Henry and I worked it together. We had a suspect . . ."

I hesitated, staring at Henry. He shook his head. "John was never convinced. It was an American chap, Brad Johnson. He was one of those white supremacy militia types. We have them over here too, but we haven't got any Rocky Mountains where we can lose them and let them play Rambo. God alone knows what he was doing over here, but we'd been keeping an eye on him because he was hooking up with a few radical far-right groups, and we were worried about possible terrorist attacks."

I took over. "It turned out he knew Sally-Anne Sterling. They had met on a dating site. Apparently, after the first date, she didn't want to know, and he got mad. He sent her a few ugly messages. When we found the emails, we went and had a talk with him. He mouthed off a lot, he was an ugly customer, but I never liked him for the murders. Henry and the rest of the team disagreed. The evidence was inconclusive. In fact, there *was* no forensic evidence —or very little . . ."

Henry said, "We found Johnson's prints at the scene, and traces of his DNA on her bedsheets . . ."

I nodded. "The forensics connected him to her, but we already knew that they were connected. What it didn't do was connect him to the *crime*, or to the other girls. He could conceivably have known them—he had no alibi for the nights of the other three killings, he was in London at the time, and he lived in the area. But none of that was enough, it was just ifs and maybes. He lawyered up, got a solicitor and a barrister, and shortly after the last killing, he returned to the U.S. After that, the killings stopped, and I returned to New York."

Henry was staring hard at me. After a moment, he grunted and said, "But he's back now."

I frowned at him. "Are you serious?"

"Deadly. We've been keeping an eye on him, but as of today I'm going to request a twenty-four-hour-a-day watch. He's been here for just over three months, promoting some business he's in or something. You were deeply invested in that case, John. You had a real feel for it."

I sighed and shook my head. "We are not going to agree, Henry. I still don't believe he's our man."

"I don't care, you are the man for this job, and I would really appreciate your help."

I hesitated. "I need to think it over."

He stared me in the eye but pointed at Dehan. "And John,

you need to discuss it with your wife. And I mean *everything*!" He drained his glass and stood. "I'm going to go and attend to a few things. I will see you back here in about three-quarters of an hour. Meanwhile, you 'fess up, me old mate."

He walked out into the leaden, gray light of the late afternoon. I could feel Dehan staring at me, but I couldn't meet her eye. Finally, she said, "What the hell is going on, Stone?"

I looked her in the eye. "I think Brad Johnson killed my wife."

CHAPTER 2

She stared at me for a long time while I stared at the large glass of dark beer on the table in front of me. Eventually, she said, "Your wife?"

I nodded, still without meeting her eye. "We were only married a very short time." I finally looked up at her. "I'm sorry. I should have told you a long time ago." She frowned, and I kept talking, trying to preempt her anger and disappointment. "There always seemed to be something else to talk about, or it was inappropriate, or it would have spoiled the mood. It's not exactly something you bring up on a honeymoon. There never seemed to be a right moment." I sighed. "Like I said, Carmen, it's not that I didn't want to tell you. I guess I've just grown used to avoiding it, not thinking about it . . . I'm sorry."

She was still frowning. "Hey."

I looked into her eyes. They were serious.

"You're my guy. Stop apologizing. I told you once, whatever it was you were not talking about, I'd hear it when you were ready. You don't need to apologize to me for anything, Stone."

She held out her fist. I smiled and punched it gently. "You're one of a kind, kiddo. I should marry you."

"So, do you still love her?"

I shrugged. "I love her memory. I always will. She was a very special person, and we were good. But it was fifteen years ago. I have laid her to rest." I shook my head. "It's not the same . . ." I gestured at her and then at me. "I'm a different person now. What we have is not like anything . . ."

She gave me a smug smile. When she spoke, her voice was quiet. "I know what we've got, Stone. You don't need to explain." Then she became serious. "But if we're going to do this, investigate this murder, you'll need to tell me what happened. You'll also have to tell me, honestly, if you *can* do it. We don't have to do this. We can go home."

I thought about it. Eventually, I gave a single nod. "Yeah, knowing you're there."

"Always."

"I met Hattie . . ." I stopped.

Dehan had given a little start. She smiled and shook her head. "It's stupid, but, realizing she had a name . . ."

"Yeah, Henrietta: Hattie. We met soon after I moved out here. We took it slow. I guess we were cautious about my job, and the fact that I lived on another continent. Plus, I was only supposed to be here six months." I paused and gave a small laugh. "We're supposed to be checking in and ordering martinis at Heathrow Airport. Instead we're here, doing this . . . You sure you're okay? It's the past. It's fifteen years ago . . ."

"Stone. Look at me . . ."

I realized I had been talking to the ceiling and sat forward to face her.

"Sometimes, when we don't confront something that we need to confront, life kicks us in the ass and *makes* us confront it."

I smiled. "Is that in the Torah?"

She nodded. "Yeah, in those very words. Exactly like that. It also says, 'Now cowboy up.'"

I sighed noisily. "After I got my first six months extended, I guess we both decided it was time to get a bit more serious and look at options. I could move here. I like England, the guys at the

Yard were getting used to me. We had a good working relationship. Henry was a friend . . ." I spread my hands. "Or, she could move back to the States with me. She wasn't crazy about that option. She was a talented artist and illustrator. She was known here, her publisher was here in London . . ."

I stopped and took a long pull on my drink.

She waited a moment, then said, "So by your seventh month here, you were beginning to get serious."

I nodded.

"You always were rash and impetuous, even back then . . . ?"

I gave her a lopsided grin. "I guess I was. So we started talking about marriage. We got engaged and I asked for a second extension, got told yes, but that was the last: either I came home or I stayed in London. We decided, whatever we did, whether we stayed in London or moved to New York, we would have to be married. So, that was what we did. I don't think her family were thrilled. A New York cop from the Bronx wasn't exactly what they had in mind for their daughter, but they accepted me."

"Was she from a nice family?"

I nodded. "What they call posh." I smiled. "Port Out, Starboard Home. That's where the first-class cabins were."

She laughed.

I went on. "She was posh, yeah. Her parents had a house in the country and another in Chelsea. We used to visit them, and with time, they grew to like me, more or less. I don't think they ever forgave me for not having a huge wedding, but Hattie told them she had better things to spend her money on, and bought me the Jag. She knew I would love it, and it was a subtle way of making it that much more difficult to go back to the States."

I fell silent. Dehan stood and went to the bar. She came back a couple of minutes later with two more pints and set one of them in front of me. It struck me that she could not have been more different from Hattie. But then, I was no longer *that* John Stone. She took a pull, smacked her lips, sighed, and smiled.

"So, meantime, almost a year has gone by. What's happening at work?"

"That was more than a year. That was about fifteen months, by the time we got married. Meantime, the killer they were now calling the Butcher of Whitechapel was turning into a real nightmare. He had killed his fourth victim, just about everybody on the task force was convinced Johnson was our man, but I didn't buy it. I don't know what it was. Maybe it was a cultural thing. They were locked into the idea that they were 'American murders.' The victims were American, serial killers are pretty rare here but common in the States, the first victim had had a relationship with an American who just reeked of killer . . ."

"But you didn't like him for it."

I shook my head. "No, because I knew he was more than capable of revenge killing, or killing some guy in a brawl in a bar, or shooting some guy in a heist. But he wasn't going to stick around to perform rituals. Johnson is just a primitive, brutish, bad man. The guy who killed these girls is a paranoid schizophrenic. Johnson, in his simple, animal way, is perfectly sane."

"So what happened?"

"There was a lot of frustration. There was no forensic evidence to move the investigation forward. We had no way of tying Johnson to any of the actual crimes. We pulled him in a few times, and each time, they either had me present at the interview or, the last couple of times, they had me interrogate him. By then, he was claiming police harassment and that we were out to frame him."

I took another pull and leaned back in my seat. "What made it more complicated was that Johnson was obviously involved in *something*. You could see that a mile away. I figured he was running small arms for radical, far-right groups over here. So that made him look guilty." I spread my hands. "Because he was. He was guilty, but he was guilty of something else."

"Did you ever prove anything, find out what he was into?"

I stared over at the cold, empty fireplace and after a while gave my head a slow shake. "No. We'd been married just a few weeks. It was about a week after I had interviewed Johnson the last time. I got home to our apartment and . . ." I had to stop. I steadied my breathing and shrugged, then shook my head. When I spoke, it came out as almost a whisper. "She'd been murdered while I was at work. In our bedroom."

We were silent for a long time. Dehan didn't speak, she just watched me. I waited for the images to subside, tried to see them in my mind as old, black-and-white photographs in an old newspaper, something that had been reported a long time ago, in another life.

I breathed slowly and steadily, and eventually I was able to talk again. "Again, there was no forensic evidence, but somebody had written on the mirror, in her blood, the words, 'back off.'"

She reached across and took my hand. "Stone, I am so sorry. I don't know what to say, what I can do . . ."

I smiled. "There is nothing anybody can do. You did it already. You married me and gave me a new life." I spread my hands, trying to stay cool and hold it together. "I went back to the States. I took the Burgundy Bruiser with me. After a couple of weeks, I went to pieces. I took three months, saw a therapist, who helped. Then I went back to work, with the determination that I would be the best cop I could be." I paused and thought a moment. "And I always had this conviction that it's not enough just to punish somebody. You have to punish them for what they have done, and they have to know that. Otherwise it is not justice, it's just revenge."

She made a face and nodded. "I get that." Then she leaned back and studied me for a moment. "Okay, so if you don't want to do this, we tell Henry and the inspector we are sorry, but it just ain't going to happen, and we go home."

"No. I do. It's . . ." I gave a one-sided shrug. "In some weird way, it's timely. It will be good to tie this up and resolve it." I gave her a smile, and couldn't keep from it fifteen years of weariness, of exhaustion from living with that nightmare ever present. "In obedience to the Torah, according to Carmen Dehan."

She smiled with rare and genuine tenderness in her huge, brown eyes. "Asshole," she said.

"You know it's mutual."

She leaned forward, with her elbows on her knees. "It's a hell of a coincidence."

"That the feeling is mutual? Not really. We are both assholes. The whole precinct knows it and agrees."

"Shut up, Stone. The fact that the girl has been killed, in the same way, and that Johnson is back in the country."

I screwed up my face and shrugged one shoulder. "It's only a coincidence if it's a coincidence, and then . . ." I nodded. "It would be *one hell* of a coincidence."

She gestured at me with an open hand. "This is either a sign that you are, truly, brilliant, or that you have been drinking too much English beer."

"I mean, if it were a coincidence, it would be one hell of a coincidence. But what if it's not? Because, you know, it probably isn't."

"That is kind of my point, Stone."

"No, I know, but think about it. Assume, for the sake of the argument, that it is not a coincidence, but also that I am right and Johnson is not our man. Where does that leave us . . . ?"

She thought about it, frowning hard. "A frame-up?"

"That's one possibility. Dehan, did you look at the note that was pinned to her eye?"

She shook her head. "I didn't know what was going on yet, and I didn't think I was invited to the party."

"Get Henry to show you. I want to know what you think. The other thing is, how tall would you say the victim was?"

She thought about it a minute. "Five two?"

"Yeah, that's what I thought."

"Shorter than the other four. Not a lot to go on."

I nodded. "I agree. Brad Johnson lives in Arizona. In a place called Three Points, west of Tucson."

"How do you know that?"

"Because I have kept a file on him for the last fifteen years, well . . . fourteen years, in fact. After I got back, I contacted Tucson PD and the sheriff of Pima County, went to see him, the sheriff, and told him the story. I told him that Scotland Yard suspected Johnson of being a serial killer, but that I thought they were wrong. I did, however, suspect him of gunrunning, and of having killed my wife. He was sympathetic, and grateful for the heads-up. He agreed to keep me in the loop if anything happened."

"And?"

"Nothing happened. So either he'd just stopped killing or he was the wrong man, as I had always suspected."

She picked up her beer and sat holding it, staring out the window at the heavy, gray light outside. Finally, she gave a small frown and said, "Or he was killing away from home."

I made a doubtful face. "Not his MO here."

She made a doubtful face to match mine, then asked, "What about the gunrunning?"

I gave a small laugh. "In Arizona, any person twenty-one years of age or older, who is not prohibited possessor, may carry a weapon, openly or concealed, without the need for a license. Arizona is one and a quarter times the size of the U.K., and has slightly less than the population of London. So, if he is buying guns in Arizona and shipping them to the U.K. on a fairly small scale, that would be hard to detect. When it comes to gunrunning, if your name is Ali, or Mustafa, and you have a big, black beard, you're probably on the radar. If you're white and blond and your name is Brad Johnson, you're probably not a member of Al-Qaeda, so nobody cares."

"So you have no hard evidence that he is or was selling guns to the U.K. far right."

"No. It was just a hunch. A strong hunch, but a hunch. He was doing something, that I am sure of. But that isn't the point."

She nodded. "I know. The point is that for fifteen years, there hasn't been another killing like those four, not near where Johnson was or here."

"Yeah, until now." I hesitated. "And the killing is similar, but it's not identical."

"Because the victim was a couple of inches shorter than the previous victims? That's pretty thin, Stone."

I sighed. "It's not just that. There are other things. Where has he been for the last fifteen years? Why has he suddenly come back, *at the same time as Johnson*? That is weird. Too weird. It's what I said to you, if you accept that it is *not* a coincidence, but also that Johnson is not the guy, where does that leave you?"

"So, hang on, hang on there a moment. What are you saying? I'm getting two things from you. You're saying you don't think Johnson did it, you never did; but you're going further. You're also saying you don't think the original killer, from fifteen years ago, did it either. You think this is a copycat."

I nodded. "I don't know if it's exactly a copycat, but this was not done by the same killer."

"How can you know? How can you be so sure? The height is not enough . . . That he was inactive for fifteen years doesn't prove anything, Stone. There could be any number of reasons for that. He might have been ill, in China, in some kind of remission— hell, he might have been in jail!"

I shook my head. "Because the original killer was probably an American, or at least he was really into Don McLean. And the man who killed that girl in Halcrow Street was English, and definitely not into Don McLean."

CHAPTER 3

BEFORE SHE COULD ASK ME ANY MORE, HENRY STEPPED through the door and approached us on heavy feet across the bare wooden floor. His eyes flicked over my face and Dehan's and he said, "I gather we have talked it all through."

I gave a single nod and stood. "Any news on the girl's ID?"

"Not much. The landlord said her name was Katie, that's all he knows . . ."

Dehan got to her feet too, frowning. "What about the rental agreement? Her name must be on that."

Henry grunted. "She paid cash, no questions asked."

We followed him to the door. As we stepped out into the leaden, gray heat, I said, "What about her accent? Was she American or British?"

"I knew you'd ask that. He said she was very posh."

Dehan asked, "That means she's British? Americans can't be posh?"

Henry laughed. I shook my head. "We can have class, but to be posh, you have to be British. It's to do with how you speak. Don't even try to understand. Just accept that it's so. She was British. More specifically, English."

"Okay, so that is out of character with the previous victims, plus she was shorter."

Henry looked at her curiously, then turned to me. "How do you feel about talking to Johnson?"

"Sure. You brought him in, or do I go get him?"

"We have nothing to bring him in on, but it might be interesting to rattle his cage. From the neighbor's testimony, we've narrowed down time of death to the last twenty-four hours. The students on the ground floor, that's the first floor to you, right? They saw her standing outside yesterday morning, smoking a cigarette."

Dehan said, "So where is this son of a bitch?"

Henry smiled at her. "He's at the Olympia, at Earl's Court. He has a stand at the Dragons, Daemons, and Dungeons exhibition." He handed her two tickets and a folded, glossy leaflet. "Enjoy." He turned to me and narrowed his eyes. "You sure about this? You want me to come along?"

"Too late for that, Henry. I'm in. But I'll be honest with you. I'm surprised they agreed to your request. I'd have serious questions about my objectivity."

"Yeah, the fact that you remarried helped. And I stressed you were only a consultant. That and the fact that nobody knows the case like you do swung it." He pulled out the keys to his car. "It's not a Jag, but it'll get you from A to B. Try to stay on the right side of the road."

"You mean the left."

"That's what I said."

We watched him run across the road, dodging the traffic, then made our way to the VW Passat he'd parked opposite the entrance to the pub. I leaned on the roof as she opened the passenger door to get in. "He's right about one thing," I said.

She jerked her head at me. "What?"

"It's not a Jag."

London has one immensely long road that runs right the way through it and all the way out to Oxford. It has various names all along its length, including High Holborn, Oxford Street, Bayswater Road, and Notting Hill Gate. We followed this road most of the way, except for Oxford Street, which is only open to big red buses and black cabs, and at Notting Hill Gate, we turned down Kensington Church Street and joined Kensington High Street. The traffic was heavy, and the humid heat was oppressive. We didn't talk, except that at one point Dehan asked me, "How do you want to do this?"

I shook my head that I didn't know. Turned to look at her and shook it again. Pretty soon, we crossed the bridge over the subway and turned right onto Olympia Way. We eventually found the multistory car park, left the car on the fourth story, and made our way on foot to the main entrance of the exhibition center. On the way I had a look at the leaflet Henry had given Dehan. It said:

SATAN'S CAVE
ONLINE STORE FOR KICK-ASS MERCHANDISE
AND MORE.

They had everything from leather cigarette pouches and customized Zippo lighters to Viking drinking horns and Confederate flags emblazoned with the skull and crossbones. There was a picture of him in one corner. He had aged, but not much. His long, sandy hair was a bit thinner on top, his beard, which had been copper, was now turning gray, but aside from that, he was pretty much the same hard-ass desperado he had been fifteen years earlier. His stall was number six six six. It kind of had to be.

We stepped through the main doors and into Geek Junction. The entire hall, which is vast, was draped in black cloth, with bits of broken castle dotted here and there. Many of the larger stalls were designed like dungeon entrances or ancient taverns from Cimmeria.

We strolled down the central aisle. I glanced at Dehan's face and smiled. She didn't look at me, she just said, "What?" and before I could answer, "Did you ever play?"

"Dragons and Dungeons? No. You did, though, didn't you?"

"You kidding? I wasn't even born when it came out."

"Yeah? I wasn't born when Clue and Monopoly came out. I still played them."

"That's different."

"Confess."

"Yeah, okay, I was addicted for, like, two years."

"It's written all over your face."

"So you're smart. Who knew."

"I am struggling not to imagine you in a brass bikini."

"Try harder. Look, there it is, over there."

We were at an intersection of two aisles. Two corners down on the left, there was a large stall, part castle wall and part bearskins. Sticking up over the corner pole was a luminous cube with the number 666 on it. Dehan looked up into my face.

"You want me to go talk to him? Get him onto the subject of gun control. How hard it is to get a piece in this country . . ."

I smiled at her. "He's a white supremacist militia man. You are half Mexican and half Jewish. How do you think that's going to work out?"

She slid her eyes sideways. "I could use the Force. I trained as a Jedi too, you know?"

"I know. But this time, let's just pay him a surprise visit."

He was crouching behind a counter that was draped with black velvet and laid on top with trays of silver rings and torques, mostly bearing either skulls, dragons, or wolves. Hanging on the back wall were samurai swords, Viking swords, and battle-axes. There were also drinking horns, flagons, and various other bits of kit for anybody bent on remembering their previous incarnation as a heroic barbarian.

I leaned on the counter and spoke quietly. "I hope you're not hiding back there, Brad."

He looked up and his eyes shifted from my face to Dehan's and back again. They said he recognized me, but he asked, "Do I know you?"

I felt a slow, hot rage begin to build in my gut, but I kept my voice quiet. "Well, that's a little rude, Brad, to kill a man's wife and not remember his face. That's not polite."

He frowned at me, then began to smile. "No, not coming to me. But you know, when you do as much whoring as I do, it's hard to keep track of every bitch you fuck and kill, and who she was married to. It's a lot to remember. Was there anything else?"

I nodded. "Yeah. Where were you between the hours of ten a.m. yesterday and ten a.m. this morning?"

He burst out laughing. "You have *got* to be kidding me, man! I do *not* believe this! I don't have to answer your fuckin' questions, man!"

I nodded, "That's true. But you know what, if I talk to my buddies at the CID about all the war games you get up to out in the wilds of Arizona, and your far-right white supremacist friends here in the U.K., they might feel like asking you a few questions themselves. Do you know how long they can hold you without charge here, Brad? Fourteen days, and upon application by a police superintendent, that can be extended indefinitely."

He shook his head, narrowing his eyes at me. "You can't do this. You ain't a cop here. I heard you went back to New York."

Dehan smiled. "You know what? I think he does remember you."

"Oh, Brad remembers me. We're old buddies. We go back a long way, don't we, Brad? Brad's the man who killed my first wife. You don't get much closer than that, do you?"

Beads of sweat had started to appear on his temples. "What the hell's going on, man? I don't know what you're talking about." He looked at Dehan. "This guy is always trying to frame me. But I never done nothin' 'cept try and make an honest living. He hates me because I'm a redneck, but hell! There ain't no shame in bein' a redneck!"

I let him run down. When he'd finished, I shrugged and said, "You know what the tragic irony of this whole thing is, Brad? I always believed you were innocent. That whole task force was convinced you were guilty, but I kept telling them, serial killing was not your scene. You might kill for an honest reason, but not just for kicks."

He looked confused. "Well, that's right. I ain't never been into that weird shit."

"So where were you, Brad? Or would you rather the anti-terrorist squad ask you?"

"Oh, man!" He heaved a big sigh. "Last night? I was at home. I got stoned with some chick and watched a movie."

"How about in the afternoon?"

"I was here, setting up the stall."

"All afternoon?"

"Yeah, all afternoon! Of course all afternoon! This is my fuckin' business. It's what I live on. What do you think I was doing the day before opening at the biggest fuckin' exhibition in Europe?"

"How about in the morning?"

"At my apartment, loading up the van, where do you think? You know, you cops make me sick! You shit and the department is there to wipe your fuckin' ass. You need a car, you need a holiday, you need a doctor, you need a fuckin' shrink. The PD is there to take care of it. Me? A regular guy like me? I have to do the whole fuckin' thing myself. And believe me, it ain't easy when some fuckin' cop has decided *you killed his fuckin' wife and one way or another you are going down for it*!"

His voice had been steadily getting louder, until his face flushed red and he shouted the last words. People turned to stare, then went on their way.

The three of us were quiet for a moment, then I said, "So what you're telling me is that you have no alibi."

He nodded. "Yeah, that's what I am telling you. And you have no evidence to put me at the scene, or instead of some crazy New York bozo and his girlfriend, they'd have English cops here putting me in cuffs. So get the hell out of my face."

Dehan said, "What scene, Brad?"

He made a face that said she was stupid. "Seriously? What

scene? What, you think you caught me out? Oh, wait, you're asking me where I was yesterday just to pass the time? Or the crime was committed in a space-time vortex so there was no *actual* scene? Get real, sister!" He shook his head and said, "Now tell me not to leave town and walk outta here like you didn't just make fuckin' assholes of yourselves."

I ignored him and asked, "Who was the girl you watched the movie with?"

"I'm going to count to three, then I'm calling security. Then I'm going to call my attorney and sue your ass!"

"Yeah, I remember you had an attorney back in the day. What was his name? You still got the same guy? Nigel? Nigel Hastings?"

"One, two . . ."

I sighed. "Okay, Brad, we're going. Just one question before we do."

"What?"

"You know Don McLean's song 'Pride Parade'?"

He screwed his face up at me like I was talking word salad at him. "What?"

"Don McLean. You know who Don McLean is?"

"Yeah, I know who fuckin' Don McLean is. What I don't know is what the fuck you are talking about. You want to get the hell out of here? I'm trying to promote my business."

I raised a hand. "Bear with me, Brad. Don McLean recorded a song in 1972 called 'The Pride Parade.'"

"So what?"

"What did you think of it?"

"Nothing. I didn't think anything of it. I don't know the fucking song. 'Pride Parade'? What is he, gay? I know he married a Jewess and he has Jewish fuckin' kids! Now stop wasting my fuckin' time and get the hell out of here!"

I smiled at Dehan. "Thanks, Brad." I winked at him. "Catch you later."

We walked back down the aisle and stepped out of the exhibition hall into the heat of the late afternoon. We fell into step, walking slowly back toward the parking garage. I pulled my cell from my pocket and checked that I had recorded our last exchange. It was all there.

Dehan said, "You want to tell me what that was all about?"

I put my hands in my pockets. "Don McLean was married for thirty years to a Jewish woman, Patrisha. Both his kids were brought up Jewish."

"Okay . . ."

"Brad Johnson is an active white supremacist and, like most white supremacists, he is also deeply anti-Semitic and buys into the whole Rothschild, Zionist conspiracy for a one-world government theory, all that crap."

"So it makes sense that he wouldn't be all that interested in . . . oh, wait . . ."

"Exactly. The guy who killed Amy, Cindy, Sally-Anne, and Kathleen clearly has an abiding interest in Don McLean."

She frowned. "And 'Pride Parade'?"

"He understandably mistook the meaning of the title, which has nothing to do with being gay. Gay used to mean happy, pride used to mean pride, now they are both associated with homosexuality, something which Brad abhors. So he asked if Don McLean was gay. Somehow, I think that our killer would not have made that mistake. Either way, the first thing that came to his mind was *not* 'American Pie.' He may be many things, but he is not our serial killer."

"What do you want to do now?"

I gave it some thought. "We go and have a talk with Henry. Let's see what he's found out about this girl, Katie. I also need to look at the file on Hattie. I've never . . ." I faltered. "I've never been able to bring myself to read the file. But I think it's time, Dehan. Maybe I have a chance here to nail the bastard and lay her to rest at last."

She nodded. "Yeah, that's a good idea. We have three crimes here, Stone, six murders and three crimes. We need to keep them clear and separate in our minds."

"I know. Three crimes and only one suspect. That's no accident."

"What do you mean?" She stopped on the corner of the parking garage. "No accident how?"

I shook my head. "I don't know yet, but I can tell you it's no accident."

I thumbed my address book and called Henry.

"John, where are you?"

"We just came out of the Olympia."

"Excellent. How did it go?"

I looked at Dehan a moment. "It was interesting. We need to talk."

"Good, come over to the embankment. I'm in my office. I'll tell them to expect you downstairs and show you up."

"Henry? I'm going to need a couple of things."

"Anything. Name it."

"I need the file on Hattie's death."

He was quiet for a moment, then said, "Okay, John, but let's not get sidetracked."

"Don't worry about it. That's not going to happen."

He didn't sound convinced. "Hang on, John, not so fast. Are you sure you're up to reading that report?"

"Yes. Just please do it, Henry."

He sighed. "Okay, if you're sure."

"I am. Another thing. The note that was pinned to Katie's eye. Have you got a copy of it?"

"Yes. Of course."

"I'm going to need that, and copies of the other four from fifteen years ago. Can you do that for me?"

I could hear him making notes. "Yes, sure," he said. "Anything else?"

"Yeah, a big bottle of Bushmills."

He laughed out loud. "Same old John Stone. I'll have it all waiting for you when you get here."

"Give me twenty minutes or half an hour."

Dehan was standing with her hands in her pockets, shaking her head at her feet. She looked up, and her face was eloquent of a curious mixture of admiration and despair. "A bottle of Bushmills? Seriously? A detective inspector of Scotland Yard asks you what you need, and John Stone, with his two king-size cojones, says, a bottle of Bushmills. You are singular and unique, Sensei. They made you and they broke the mold."

I gave a small laugh and started to walk again toward the entrance of the parking garage. "It's not as outrageous as you might think, Little Grasshopper. There is, as the old cliché would have it, a method to my madness."

"You have a reason for asking Scotland Yard to provide you with a bottle of Bushmills."

I nodded. "I prefer it to Scotch. It is distilled three times, so it's smoother. And did you know that the ten-year-old single malt is matured in bourbon casks as well as oloroso sherry casks?"

She took my arm in both of hers and rested her head on my shoulder. "Nope, I didn't know that, Sensei. You are my source of useless information in shining armor."

"You are impertinent, Dehan."

"Will you punish me?"

"See?"

"With handcuffs?"

"See? Impertinent."

Scan the QR code below to purchase THE BUTCHER OF WHITECHAPEL.
Or go to: righthouse.com/the-butcher-of-whitechapel

Made in United States
Cleveland, OH
04 December 2025

27504958R00132